# AN INKLING OF EVIL

KALLI BALLAS MYSTERY
BOOK 4

## KARI LEE TOWNSEND

*This one goes out to my own crazy extended family. We might not be Greek, but the Townsend, Harmon, Hutteman, and Denny descendants sure do know how to have fun. Cheers to family traditions, health, and happiness.*

# PRAISE FOR THE KALLI BALLAS MYSTERY SERIES

"Townsend once again introduces us to unforgettable characters in this first book of her new Kalli Ballas Mystery series. The scenes with Kalli's family will give you flashbacks to 'My Big Fat Greek Wedding', with family members you hope you'll see again. Once she meets Nik and his slobbering St. Bernard, you're going to wonder how in the world is our germaphobe-sleuth going to team up with the detective to clear her best friend's name? But Kalli has a secret she's learning to live with and using this newfound gift means she's going to have to curb her OCD and touch strangers in order to read their minds. The fate of her best friend is in her very capable, very sanitized hands."

— *TOP AMAZON REVIEWER*

"What a fun and funny cozy mystery! It's filled with wonderful, sometimes over-the-top characters (of course they are mostly Greek so how could you expect anything else?), danger, suspense, plenty of suspects and red herrings, and mysteries that kept me guessing until the end. Kalli is sweet and quirky with her OCD, germaphobia, and her ability to hear thoughts with just a touch. Nik is her dreamy next door neighbor, a police officer, and he happens to be crazy about Kalli. The possible romance building between them is so entertaining to watch. Now if scheming ex's, interfering family, and bad guys could just leave them alone they might actually get to go on a first date. Highly recommend."

*— TOP AMAZON REVIEWER*

"Kalli Ballas thought she had a chance at a relationship with Detective Nik Stevens until his ex-girlfriend shows up claiming to be pregnant with his baby. To make matters worse, the ex-girlfriend is found murdered in Nik's mother's kitchen. Kalli finds herself working with Nik to find the real killer and clear his mother's name. I had to laugh at Kalli's germaphobia and her obsession with hand sanitizer. To find the killer, Kalli has to use her ability to read a person's thoughts just by touching them and then find a creative way to pass the information along while keeping her ability a secret. I loved the wonderful Greek characters and the Greek traditions throughout the book. I just hope there are more books in this series!"

*— TOP AMAZON REVIEWER*

"This is a hilarious cozy mystery. The characters are wildly Greek and has all the big family drama that involves lots of food and talking. Kalli is adopted (non-Greek) OCD and germophobic. She is also able read people's minds when she touches them. Nik is a half-Greek detective who lives next door to Kalli. The story has a lot of laugh out loud moments as the elders try to mold the children to their will. The plot is very well laid out as the author is able to keep the identities of the perpetrators from the readers until the reveal. It is also romantic as Kalli and Nik work to build a relationship that is torn apart by drama."

— TOP AMAZON REVIEWER

"Excellent third book in the Kalli Ballas Mystery series. There's plenty of mystery, danger, intrigue, shady dealings, romance, quirkiness, laughter, teasing of the pole, and a Greek ma doing everything she can to protect her beloved adopted daughter from her shifty biological mom who shows up out of the blue...with her hand out. I couldn't put it down until I was done."

— TOP AMAZON REVIEWER

"This little town was just full of mysteries, suspects, motives and secrets. I couldn't put it down because it pulled me into the story and I had to see what happened next. I loved the characters, the many twists and turns this story took, and how it kept me guessing. Excellent read!"

— TOP AMAZON REVIEWER

"A fun cozy mystery with Kalli and Nik and their big Greek family. Kalli is a germaphobe who can also read the minds of the people she is touching. Her boyfriend Nik is a police detective. It is great fun as her mother is accused of murder and they set out to try and solve the case. There are fumbles and mishaps that will make you laugh."

**1**

"Well, Detective Dreamy, we made it through half the holiday season, and we're still together," I said loudly to my *official* boyfriend, Nikos Stevens, before taking a sip of my eggnog. I could barely hear myself think above the booming music, stomping, clapping, and plate smashing.

"Cheers to that, Ballas." He clinked glasses with mine and took a hearty sip of his own. He was so handsome. Well over six-feet-tall with thick wavy coffee-colored hair, olive skin, piercing blue eyes, and a heavily whiskered face.

I inhaled deep and tried not to swoon. He smelled amazing: buttered rum, cinnamon, spice, and something uniquely him. He held my hand and kissed my cheek. *You smell amazing, too, Kalliope.* He winked. I squeezed his hand and smiled a little before letting go.

Nik couldn't read minds like I could, but he could read *me* like a book.

Apparently, I wore my emotions all over my face. But ever since he'd found out that I fell and hit my head and could suddenly read minds when touching someone, he used every opportunity to occupy my thoughts. He loved letting me know exactly what he was thinking at the most inopportune moments.

Trust me, I wasn't complaining.

Hearing his thoughts was the only way I could have a semi-normal romantic relationship with a man. Being a germaphobe with quirks didn't make dating easy for me. I could never get out of my head long enough to fall for a guy. Thanks to my ability and a man who made me lose my mind completely, I was finally living the life I'd always dreamed of but never thought I could have. Although, that life came with a whole lot of baggage on both our sides.

Both of our big, fat, Greek families went over the top during the holidays, and our Greek mamas were thrilled we were an official couple this year. Since neither family wanted to miss out on having us with them for literally every event, they'd teamed up together for *twice the fun*, according to them.

More like twice the chaos for Nik and me.

Tonight was my parents' annual holiday party, held at their Greek restaurant, Aphrodite's. Their usual ancient Athens décor, with marble statues scattered about, filled every possible vacant spot in the large room. During the holidays, they decked out the restaurant and even adorned the statues with ribbons and bows.

Greek families traditionally decorate a boat instead of a tree at Christmas time. They want to celebrate Saint Nicholas, patron saint of sailors, and his connection to the sea in honor of sailors returning home to their families. The boats are decorated with lights from December sixth until January sixth through Christmas Eve, New Year's Eve, and Epiphany.

My parents proudly displayed an eight-foot dinghy

in the corner of the restaurant, with blue and white lights like the Greek flag, tinsel, garland, and ornaments. They kept the bow pointed inwards toward the center of the room, symbolizing the homeward journey.

Of course, my family had to do everything over the top, even for the Greek's.

Pop placed a giant bag of Santa's toys in the center of the boat. In true dramatic Ballas fashion, he had even rigged up a giant-sized dolphin stuffed animal to the front of the boat and painted his nose red.

His version of Rudolph aka Ru-dolphin.

Ma made homemade outfits for her and Pop to dress up as Santa and Mrs. Claus. All the children and grandchildren took turns climbing into the boat to take pictures. My life was a continuous episode of the Twilight Zone, but I wouldn't trade it for anything. After all I had gone through with my birth mother and finally meeting my birth father, I had come to embrace my adoptive Greek family.

They were even making plans to adopt my fully grown half-brother, Jasper Kent.

Jasper had the same green eyes as me and our mother, but he looked more Greek than I did with his dark hair and tanned skin, clearly taking after his father—whoever that was. He had been in the foster system from the age of five but didn't get lucky like I did. So, even though he was twenty-seven, he was fully on board with becoming part of the Ballas family, and Ma was over the moon, trying to make up for lost time.

"Frona, put that down." My short, plump YiaYia Dido with her long gray hair in her standard bun and ever-present apron tied around her waist ran after my cousin.

Frona bounced around the room on a pogo stick with the baby Jesus from the manger strapped to her back. "Jingle bells, baby smells, Ru-dolphin swam away," she sang over and over, her cockeyed pigtails bouncing to the beat.

She'd fallen off an apple cart when she was a child and had never been the same, but she was happy. She worked as a dishwasher in my parents' restaurant, and her sister Eleni worked as a waitress. Leni had waist length dark curly hair and was one of the most eligible bachelorettes in Clearview.

But tonight, everyone was there to enjoy the party and not work.

Nik's ma was there, hobbling about on crutches after falling on the ice. She'd needed knee surgery and Captain Quincy Crenshaw had been by her side every step of the way, doting on her. Aunt Tasoula was there with her latest man, Tate Hemsworth, who happened to be Ma's ex from high school. Nik's cousin Thalia and my cousin Leni were both still single and ready to mingle. The problem was they were related to half the town since both of our families made up a considerable amount of its citizens.

There weren't many fish left in Clearview's sea.

"Why you two stand in corner?" Ma asked Nik and me, her big poof of teased black hair more impressive than ever. She smoothed her flashy polyester pantsuit before adding, "Go make merry. You no happy?"

"I value my life, Ma," I said, watching Aunt Tasoula take a shot of Ouzo and shout, "Opa!" before smashing a plate, her way-too-long hair and too-tight clothes drawing more attention than the flying pieces of porcelain.

The smashing of plates was a famous Greek tradition. When people were having a great time, they smashed plates to show their joy and appreciation for the music being played. If there had been live entertainment, the guests would toss flowers. Tonight, it was all about the plates.

At my parents' restaurant, all bets were off.

"Value, Schmalue...it's tradition." Ma talked with her hands, her beehive of hair swaying with every word.

"Hi, Ophelia, thank you so much for inviting me to the party. I've never been to anything like this before," Jasper said as he came to a stop by Ma.

"You call me Ma. You *my* son now." She patted his chest and then swiped her hand through the air. "That's that."

Jasper looked at me with raised brows. I knew he felt like he was intruding on my family, but he wasn't. I was happy to have a sibling, and I could tell he wanted to be a part of our family more than anything. I smiled and winked at him, and then he relaxed.

"Now go eat. You too skinny." Ma shooed him away.

"I don't want to be a glutton. You have other guests."

"Bah. They family, not guests. You Greek now. We Greeks *never* run out of food. Now go join your cousins by the food table. Shoo shoo."

I laughed. "Don't try to fight it. You won't win."

"She's right, man." Nik rubbed his over-full stomach and groaned.

"Well, all right, then." Jasper walked away with steps lighter than anytime I had seen him since we first met.

Delilah Doolittle, our local party planner, carried a stack of dessert plates as she stopped by Ma. "I'm so sorry to interrupt, but I wanted to let you know the cake is here." She leaned in close. "I have to say it's a work of art."

Delilah was a petite strawberry-blonde woman with catlike pale-green eyes. A bubbly dynamo of a woman who was great at her job. She had her assistant, Cameron Oswald, special order a themed cake that was a replica of my parents' restaurant, right down to the last detail, with the Christmas boat displayed as well. The owner's men had damaged the original masterpiece when setting it up that morning, so the Cake King had personally recreated the cake and was setting it up himself, with Cameron's help.

"It should be a work of art for what I'm paying." Ma nodded once. "Tell him I'll be back in a minute."

Delilah nodded and started to leave when the front door burst open.

The music stopped and everyone stared, wide eyed. Even Frona stopped bouncing. My parents' holiday party was closed to the public. Everyone knew that. My mind drifted away from that thought and locked onto the spectacle playing out before me.

A man stood in the doorway with his legs spread wide apart and his hands on his hips. He had to be six-foot-five with shoulders that filled the entrance. His shoulder-length, dark-blond hair fell in waves, and his bright blue eyes that looked oddly familiar sparkled as they scanned the room, as if searching for someone.

"Dibs!" shouted Leni and Thalia simultaneously, then they rolled their eyes. The last time they had fought over a guy, it hadn't ended well.

"Who is that?" Aunt Tasoula asked in barely more than a whisper.

Ma frowned. "You already have a man. This new guy is half your age."

"Age, schmage," my aunt breathed in awe. "I might be taken, but I no blind."

"It's that Thor in the movies," someone said.

"No, no. It's that famous Viking, Ragnar," someone else said.

"No. It's the romance hero, Fabio, I tell you," someone else chimed in.

Chloe's eyes widened in disbelief, and she nearly tripped over her crutches. "Uh, oh."

Nik set his jaw. "You're all wrong. That's no hero... that's my cousin, Viggo."

So that was why the giant's blue eyes looked familiar. He was obviously from Nik's non-Greek side of the family. I didn't know much about Nik's father's side of the family, but one thing I did know...

Nik did *not* look happy to see him.

"You two live together?" Viggo asked as we pulled into the driveway of the big white house we shared.

"No," we both answered simultaneously.

"Ahhhh, I see." Viggo sat in the front seat of Nik's car because he was too big for the back. He craned his head around on that big neck of his and ogled me. "Then that means you're available, right?"

My eyebrows shot straight up into my hairline, and my mouth fell open. It was the cold and flu season, and the air in the car felt stagnate. I could feel the germs soaring into my lungs, and I started coughing. That couldn't be good.

"That would be a definite no," Nik ground out through his teeth, shooting me a questioning glance in the rear-view-mirror when I hesitated.

"Definitely no!" I concurred and then cleared my

throat. "We are an *official* couple," I quickly clarified, trying to reassure him but sounding ridiculous to myself.

Poor Nik had waited forever for me to get over my fears and agree to be official. I didn't want him to think I had eyes for the giant beside him like half the town. Detective Dreamy was the only god/romance hero/Viking I would ever need or want.

"Official?" Viggo eyed me curiously.

"The point is we're both off the market, and that's that." I swiped my hand through the air, taking a page out of Ma's book.

"We each have our own apartments in this house." Nik cut the engine and looked at his cousin. "You'll be staying with me and me alone. Am I clear?"

Viggo held up his massive hands. "Hands off the hottie. Got it."

Nik frowned.

Viggo winked.

I blushed.

"I'm going to change, and I'll be over in a minute." I scrambled out of the car.

"It's okay if you don't come over. You're probably tired," Nik said to me as he stepped out of the car as well.

"Not at all. I'm wide awake." I leaned in and kissed his cheek, whispering for his ears only, "This *hottie* isn't missing a single word." I stepped back and blew him a kiss.

He rolled his eyes and smirked at me then led the way inside his half of the house with the big, strapping Viking behind him. I hadn't thought I would ever meet someone bigger than Nik, but Viggo was a beast. I crinkled my brow. Beasts were scary and caused trouble. Something told me crashing the plate smashing party was only the beginning when it came to Nik's Casanova cousin.

Ten minutes later, after I'd changed into yoga pants and a fuzzy sweater and gave Miss Priss, my finicky calico cat, some cuddles, I let myself into Nik's apartment. Heavy cologne filled the entrance way, assaulting my senses, undoubtedly killing any lingering germs. The man hadn't smelled like that in the car. He must have reapplied after getting here.

Why? We weren't going anywhere.

Unless he planned to slip out and cause even more chaos. Anything was possible with Casanova. I made my way to the kitchen where Nik and Viggo sat, having a beer. Wolfgang, Nik's massive slobbery Saint Bernard, spotted me and sprang to his feet, his entire body wiggling. I held up my hand, and he flopped his fanny down on the floor. We'd come to a certain understanding. If he behaved, then I would pet the top of his head.

And then scrub my hands thoroughly, of course.

I walked over to Wolf, gave him an extra pet for being a good boy, and then pulled out my ever-present hand sanitizer to scrub my palm before taking a seat at the table. Nik got up and poured me a glass of chardonnay. He kept a bottle just for me at his place, and I kept beer at my place just for him.

"So, what did I miss?" I asked and took a sip.

"I was just thanking my cousin for putting me up. The Clearview Motel is full." Viggo took a chug of his beer, and half the bottle disappeared.

"It's the holidays. You have to plan ahead," Nik said. "What are you doing here, anyway? Won't Uncle Magnus and Aunt Freya be missing you back in Norway?"

"Nah, I saw my far and mor before Christmas. Now

they're headed to Britain to be with your far, Uncle Bjorn, and his new wench for New Year's Eve."

"You and I haven't spoken in years." Nik narrowed his eyes, studying his cousin. "Why come see me now?"

"My detective cousin, always so suspicious." Viggo sighed.

Nik raised a brow and scoffed. "With good reason."

There was a palpable tension humming between the two men. Nik had never mentioned Viggo, so I had no clue what had happened in the past. Whatever it was had caused bad blood between them. But I knew Nik well. Family was family, no matter what. There was no way he would leave him stranded without a place to stay.

"Clearview, Connecticut is only an hour from New York City. I was there on a modeling shoot. We wrapped up early, so I thought, why not go see my cousin and Aunt Chloe. It's been too long."

"Hmmm," was all Nik said, his voice laced with suspicion.

"Who knows. Maybe I'll find a wench of my own. I need to relax and relieve some tension." Viggo's eyes slid over to me, and the corners of his lips tipped up slightly.

He didn't miss his cousin. He was clearly messing with him.

Wolfgang growled.

"Watch yourself, cuz." Nik's tone held a note of steel, and I'd never seen his eyes so intensely scary. "My hospitality only goes so far."

"Look, I'm not here to cause trouble. I really do want to catch up with both you and your mor."

"*Ma* doesn't need any drama," Nik said, his Greek roots showing over his Scandinavian. "She got enough of that from Pop. This is *my* town, Viggo, and it's the holidays. Behave yourself, and we won't have any problems."

"Done. Now if you don't mind, can I borrow your car? The Suburban I rented broke down as soon as I got here. I'm at your mercy until it gets fixed."

"It's after midnight. Where are you going?"

"You know I've always been a night owl." Viggo wagged his eyebrows. "I saw a cool pub in town I want to check out."

"That would be Flannigan's Pub." Nik tossed Viggo his keys and checked his watch. "Better hurry. They close at two."

Viggo saluted the two of us and headed towards the door, saying over his shoulder, "That'll do. And if not, I'm sure I can find something to do with my time." He closed the door behind him.

"And that, *cuz*, is what I'm afraid of."

**2**

---

The next morning, I picked up our breakfast order from Maria Danza's bakery, Sinfully Delicious, and crossed the street to Full Disclosure. My best friend, Jazlyn Alvarez, owned the clothing boutique and let me use her loft upstairs to create my designs for my Kalli Originals lingerie line.

Maria was a feisty Italian with long black hair and cherubic cheeks, while Jaz was an exotic, tall goddess with thick honey-brown curls and amber eyes. They used to be enemies because Jaz had all the men in town after her until she finally admitted Nik's partner, Detective Boomer Matheson, was the love of her life.

Boomer wasn't Jaz's usual type of a big, blond, bombshell. He was tall and lean with russet colored hair, hazel eyes, and wore a brown leather jacket with jeans most days. While Jaz was an exotic goddess who liked to be in control and order her men around. Boomer was having none of that, and Jaz had finally met her match.

A man who challenged her.

With Jaz officially off the market, delivery man, Sully Anderson, stopped pining after her and discovered what was right in front of him. He and Maria had been going strong ever since, and Jaz and Maria had called a truce. I, for one, was grateful because Jaz got hangry when she wasn't fed first thing in the morning, and baked goods were her favorite.

Sugar and caffeine.

I shuddered just thinking about the order I carried in my hands. I'd tried to tell her many times what all that sugar was doing to her insides, but I'd learned to keep my mouth shut if I wanted to keep the peace. Meanwhile, I had a healthy stash of organic whole foods in my loft to go with my herbal tea.

"There you are," Jaz said the second I walked through the front door. She snatched the cup of coffee I held, took a big gulp, and then sighed. "Thank you, my friend, you're a life saver."

Debbie, the fashion designer intern she'd hired, who was now a full-time employee, sat on a throw pillow on a stool behind the register, getting her drawer ready to cash people out. Jaz had taught her every aspect of the fashion business. She both designed and bought inventory for the store, and it was nice to have the help since Jaz's business had grown.

There was a burgundy microfiber sofa in the sitting area next to the dressing rooms, with decorative pin-striped pillows and a matching loveseat filled with early shoppers already. Soft music played through the sound system, and the boutique smelled of lavender.

I secretly sanitized the furniture every chance I got, even though Jaz had a cleaning crew. At least my loft studio was spotless, just the way I liked it, with a hand sanitizer stand at the top of the stairs just in case. My only request was that no one was allowed up there. When it came to my sanctuary, I was particular, and Jaz had been gracious enough to give me free reign.

"Are Chanel and Versace still getting you up early?" I asked.

Jaz and Boomer had adopted the purebred full-size black poodles, who had more bling than Nelson Rockwell's jewelry store. But even I had to admit, they were way better behaved than either Nik's Saint Bernard or my calico cat. They were just early risers because of their former owners.

"You have no idea. And Boomer just sleeps through it all." She shook her head. "I can't imagine what it's going to be like when we have kids."

My eyes sprang wide. "Did he ask you to marry him?" Jaz and Boomer had just gotten back from vacation, and we hadn't had a chance to get caught up yet.

"Not yet." She winked. "But Loverboy will. It's only a matter of time."

I just laughed. Leave it to Jaz to put the cart before the horse. I flipped through the stock of my lingerie on display, mentally taking note of what needed to be swapped out with the new inventory of my winter line.

"Speaking of lover boys...the rumor mill has been buzzing all morning about a godlike Viking romance hero who has turned this town upside down in just one night." She rubbed her hands together. "The rumor mill also said he was seen outside your parents' restaurant. I want details, darling."

I groaned. "Viggo Stevens."

"Wait..." Her eyes widened. "*Stevens*?"

I nodded. "Nik's cousin."

"But I heard he's blond, and Nik's so Greek."

"Half-Greek, remember? Viggo is Nik's cousin on his father's side. The Viking's from Norway."

"Just listen to the words coming out of your mouth. The Viking's from Norway. That sounds larger than life, like something right out of the movies."

"Trust me, you haven't seen Viggo yet. He *is* larger than life. He's a model and Nik said he's starred in some commercials and a few low budget movies. I have to admit, even I was a little starstruck, which didn't go over very well with *my* lover boy." I lifted my hands. "Nik has the same eyes and he's a big man for a half-Viking, but the purebreds are enormous."

"Wow, your Detective Dreamy comes from some pretty spectacular genes: both mythological and legendary." She puckered her brow. "But I thought his father was from Britain?"

"That's where he lives now, but he was born and raised in Norway."

"The goblins are up to no good again!" Ma came bursting through the door, out of breath and frazzled.

Kallikantzaroi were mischievous Greek goblins that came up to the surface of the Earth at the end of December, during the twelve days of Christmas, causing all sorts of trouble and mischief. They didn't leave until the winter solstice was done on January sixth. I didn't believe in such things, but Ma and Aunt Tasoula blamed everything that went wrong during the holidays on the goblins.

Jasper didn't have a clue what it was like to be part of my family, but he would soon.

"What happened this time, Ma?"

"They're all gone. No more Christmas treats." She swiped her hand through the air. "I made a double batch of snowy Kourabiethes, Melomakaranas, Diples, and Baklava. No cookies left. Just a stinky restaurant. Nobody gonna come eat in a stinky place with crumbs."

"Are you sure it's not just Pop and Papou Homer messing with you?" I asked gently. "They both love your sweets and have been known to stink after over-indulging."

"Bah! I know who it is. It's the goblin Katachanas. He no stop eating everything in sight, and he stinks something awful." She waved her hand in front of her nose.

"So, I'm taking it our lunch date is off?"

"That's what I say. No lunch date. You no listen." Ma shook her head. "I have to start all over again. I told Papa to burn a large log for twelve days. Then they no come down my chimney. But you pop no listen, either. He always too busy. Maybe I be too busy for him now." She threw her hands up in the air, leaving in a flurry just like the way she came in, with an additional string of Greek curse words following her out the door.

I let out a long sigh, saying the only thing left to be said...

"And so it begins."

~

THE RUMOR MILL was ramping up speed. Viggo's first night in town, and he had already slept with a married woman. He was making as many enemies as friends, and my poor Detective Dreamy had his hands full trying to keep the peace.

Jaz and I were having lunch at my cousins Kosmos and Silas's deli, Diner Delights, where Kosmos made the orders and Silas ran the register. Kosmos had dark cropped hair. He was short, built like a tank, and tough as nails, but his dreamy bedroom eyes gave him away. He might act all quiet and brooding, but he was a softy on the inside.

Winnie Wallabe, our Australian mail carrier, had

seen right through him. She was a tall redhead, full of sass and spunk. They couldn't be more opposite, but they'd been inseparable since she'd gotten out of the hospital.

Nearly dying will do that to people.

Meanwhile, his brother Silas was thin and tall, with curly black hair, dimples, and the biggest flirt in Clearview. Or he was, anyway, before he met the new bartender at Flannigan's Pub. Zena Renner, a short blonde pixie with lavender eyes, a big smile, and an even bigger personality, had stolen his heart.

Like Jaz, he'd also finally met his match.

"What's that mysterious smile for?" Jaz asked, eating her Italian sandwich that Kosmos always made for her, even though their diner was Greek.

I sat across from her at our table, eating my gyro. "I'm just happy my cousins have both found someone special." My smile slipped when my gaze landed on my other cousin, Yanni, who sat at a table alone. He had his own landscaping business and was laser focused on growing that, not interested in a relationship. I worried about him being alone forever.

"If only Yanni could find someone." I nodded discreetly in his direction. "He's the oldest of us all and so serious. All he ever does is work."

"Oh, I don't know. That doesn't look like work to me." Jaz pointed at the woman who had just walked through the door.

Dixie Doolittle was the twin sister of Delilah, the party planner. They were identical: petite with strawberry blonde hair and green eyes. The only difference was that Delilah was more sophisticated in the way she talked and dressed, where Dixie was more down-to-earth and casual. She was an antique collector and owned a cute little shop in town. She looked around the room, spotted Yanni, and headed straight toward his table.

I sat up straight. "Maybe you're right."

She sat down, smiled, and shook Yanni's hand. His lips remained unsmiling, and he nodded once all businesslike before he pulled out a book of his landscaping designs.

"Or maybe not," Jaz said. "That man needs to learn to relax and have fun."

The bells above the door rang again, and in walked Detective Dreamy and Viggo the Viking. They placed their order and headed in our direction, parting the sea of oohs and aahs pouring out of the gaping mouths of women and men.

"Whoa..." Jaz's mouth fell open to match the mesmerized townsfolk around her, and then she choked on a piece of sandwich.

"Told you so." I missed my mouth with my straw twice before taking a sip of my iced tea.

Nikos was well over six feet and Viggo was a couple inches taller than him. Both were equally impressive. Nik's face was chiseled and unsmiling beneath his dark, heavy five o'clock shadow as he locked intense blue eyes on me and made strong purposeful strides in our direction, not breaking eye contact even once.

Meanwhile, Viggo strode casually beside him, his blond hair blowing as if a wind machine from one of his modeling shoots was aimed at him. His eyes locked onto Jaz, tracing over her face, then crinkling as his full lips tipped up slowly at the corners. His glittering blue eyes and clean-shaven face made him look like an angel, but he was no angel...

His charming ways got him into devilish trouble daily.

Nik had clearly reached his limit for patience, judging by his expression.

"Hello, ladies," Viggo said, his deep voice rivalling a baritone opera singer, striking just the right chords.

A sigh slipped Jaz's lips, but I was smart enough to swallow mine.

Nik frowned.

Jaz fanned her face.

Viggo grinned.

I smiled overly wide. "Have a seat." I gestured toward the other chairs at our table a little too emphatically.

"I thought you were having lunch with your ma?" Nik sat beside me, pulling his chair closer than usual.

"Goblins."

"Ah, enough said." Nik shook his head. "Captain Crenshaw has been living off take-out because Ma swears Magaras has been in her house. She keeps throwing all the food she makes out after a single sniff test. Captain says he doesn't smell anything, but he's learned pretty quickly that you can't argue with a Greek mama."

"Who is Magaras?" Jaz's eyebrows drew together.

"A Greek goblin with a big fat drum-like belly who leaves terrible, filthy smells all over people's food," I explained.

"Your people have some strange traditions," Viggo said, then ate the second half of his sandwich in one bite. "Speaking of Aunt Chloe, I'd like to see her today."

"If you think you can stay out of trouble long enough, I can arrange that." Nik left most of his sandwich untouched, concentrating on his strong black coffee and rubbing one temple instead.

"Look, it's not my fault. The lass didn't tell me she

was married. She came up to me, not the other way around. I was simply being a gentleman and obliging the lady."

"Well, that *lady* happens to be married to a lumberjack who knows how to use a chainsaw. Mack Finley is not exactly someone you want to mess with."

"Have you seen the size of me, cousin?"

"I repeat...*chainsaw*."

Viggo shrugged. "I'm familiar with chainsaws. I was on a modeling shoot for a logging company one time."

"That's not the same." Nik sighed. "I asked you not to stir up trouble while you're in town, and you can't even last one night. You're lucky the hotel manager called me, and I got there in time to intercept Mack before he returned from his truck. It's the holidays, Vig. No one needs drama right now."

Viggo barked out a laugh. "Said the Greek whose mama sees goblins."

Nik's face hardened. "I can send you packing any time. The only reason I haven't is because of Aunt Freya." He looked him in the eye. "She called, worried about you. What's really going on?"

Viggo lost his smug smile. "I've been going through some things. No big deal." His eyes met Nik's. "Thank you, cuz. I really will try to do better. I mean it. I need this trip." He paused a beat. "I really need to see Aunt Chloe."

Nik lost his scowl and nodded. "Okay, then." He finished his coffee and looked at his watch. "This is probably as good a time as any to see Ma."

"So nice to meet you," Jaz finally said, still half in a daze.

"Likewise," Viggo responded sincerely.

So the man could be genuine and sincere when he

wanted to. I had a feeling Viggo's flirtatious mannerisms were all an act to cover a vulnerability. What that was, remained to be seen.

The men started to get up when the front door burst open.

A gorgeous woman more stunning than even Jaz marched inside, scanned the room, and then locked eyes with Viggo. The look in her eyes was downright scary. She looked obsessed or possessed. I wasn't sure there was much of a difference in this case.

"Who on earth is that?" Jaz asked.

"Drama with a capital D," Viggo said with a frown.

"Just great." Nik groaned.

"What do you want, Zelda?" Viggo asked on a weary sigh then closed his eyes for a moment as he rubbed his temples.

"How dare you walk out on me like that. After all we've been through. I deserve better, darling." She stood tall in a mink coat, her thick golden blonde locks cascading over her shoulders in waves.

"I don't owe you anything. I've told you over and over that we were only having fun. We were never an *official* couple." His eyes flickered to me before returning to her. "It's not my fault you won't take no for an answer."

"Men don't leave me." She narrowed her gorgeous lavender eyes, her full lips flattening into a single line. "You know we were more than friends."

The front door flew open again, and this time a beautiful man with glowing olive skin and slicked back black hair walked in. His eyes brightened when he spotted Zelda, then hardened when they landed on Viggo.

Viggo rolled his eyes. "What are you doing here, Knox?"

"That photo shoot should have been mine." He slapped his chest as he marched toward Viggo. "For you to bail on everyone early was so unfair. Why do you think Zelda is here? The company dropped our agency, all because of you."

"You left early?" Nik asked, drawing his eyebrows together. "You told me you wrapped up your modeling shoot."

Knox let out a disgusted snort.

Zelda let out a harsh laugh.

Jaz gasped.

I pressed my lips together to remain silent.

"I can explain," Viggo said, holding up his hands towards Detective Stevens—as Nik was most definitely in full detective mode now.

"Start talking, cuz. Now is definitely *not* the time to remain silent."

Looked like the goblins weren't the only ones set on causing trouble and mischief.

3

Nik, Viggo, and I sat at Chloe's kitchen table two days later for tea and biscuits...or in Chloe's case, lattes and Mosaiko—chocolate biscuits. Viggo had talked, all right. He'd talked in circles, not making any sense. He kept changing his story as to why he'd left the modeling shoot early. He'd said he thought they had the holiday off. Then he'd said he was fired. Then he'd finally said he needed some time off for his mental health and had cleared it with the agency.

The Dramatic Duo said he was lying.

They left, promising the drama wasn't over with yet, and they weren't kidding. Everywhere Viggo went, Zelda and Knox showed up and caused a big scene, putting a damper on the holiday festivities. They were *worse* than the goblins, and I hadn't thought that was possible.

"Why are you sweating, Viggo? It's winter." Nik's ma eyed Viggo with narrowed eyes and a pinched brow.

"I'm not sweating...am I?" Viggo wiped his forehead and frowned. "Oh." His shoulders slumped.

She felt his head with the back of her hand. "Freya

will not be happy with me if I let her baby get sick on my watch."

Viggo shrugged. "I'm a big guy, Aunt Chloe. Perspiring is natural."

I watched the scene unfold in amazement. Nik had shown me pictures of his father and Uncle Magnus. They all looked alike. That had to be hard on Chloe, being reminded of her ex every time she saw her nephew, yet she adored Viggo. According to Nik, she and his mother had remained good friends even after Chloe's divorce, and they treated each other's only sons as if they were their own.

I didn't have to be a mind reader to feel Detective Dreamy's annoyance.

"I'm more worried about you," Viggo said to his aunt, his brow furrowing. "How's your knee? My mor said you fell and had to have surgery. Are you in a lot of pain?"

"A little bit," Chloe admitted, shifting in her chair and adjusting her propped leg with a wince.

"Seeing you in pain is like seeing my mor in pain. I don't like it. Didn't they give you anything to help?"

"Yes, but I don't need pills. I'm Greek." She waved her hand in front of her face. "I don't need help. I'm tough. It's you I'm worried about. You're a big teddy bear."

"I'm not sick, I promise." Viggo's brow wrinkled. "I just have a lot going on in my life right now."

Nik snorted.

Chloe frowned. "Nikos! Manners, please." When he was Nik, he was a nice guy. When he was Detective Stevens, he was all business. When he was Nikos, he was one stubborn, arrogant Greek.

Nikos' face lost its smug expression as he grumbled, "What? At least I'm letting him stay with me."

"About that..." Viggo gave Chloe a pleading look. "Is there any chance I can stay with you while I'm here? I might be a big guy, but I'm a lover not a fighter. I need a place to meditate and work through some things. Cuz has too many distractions between his beast of a dog and his quirky girlfriend."

"Hey." My jaw fell open.

"No offense." Viggo shrugged.

*Offense taken,* I wanted to say but kept quiet.

Nik raised a brow. "I haven't heard you complain once, *cuz.*"

"Well, now that I have an obsessed woman and her crazy jealous partner-in-crime hounding me, I need a calm, quiet place to chill until I figure out what to do." Viggo threw his hands up in the air.

"Of course, you can." Chloe patted his hand. "You stay as long as you need, but I have to warn you, it's not so quiet around here this time of year." She shook her head with angry eyes. "That long-nosed Paroritis showed up just this morning before the rooster crows. He can mimic people's voices perfectly. I could have sworn Quincy was in my bed, but I open my smiling eyes, and he no there." She swiped her hand through the air.

"All right, all right." Nik held up his hand. "I don't need to hear that."

"Well, thank you, Aunt Chloe. Goblins are the last things I'm worried about." Viggo wiped his brow once more and then excused himself to use the bathroom.

We all watched him leave, and I could tell by their faces, they thought the same thing I did... Something was off with Viggo Stevens, and maybe it was time we got to the bottom of it before more damage could be done.

～

TWO DAYS LATER, it was New Year's Eve. I sighed with relief. The madness was almost over with. Both Nik's family and mine kept with many of the Greek holiday traditions. I'd stopped by my parents' restaurant, Aphrodite's, for lunch and shook my head over the overly large pomegranate hanging over the door. As soon as the New Year's Eve party was over, they would smash it. The bigger, the better, because the more seeds that spilled out, the more luck they would have for that year.

Nik's ma had hung a large sea onion known as skeletoura above her door, wrapping the bulb in foil. It was a means to worship the god of the wilds and nature known as Pan. As soon as the New Year's Eve party was over, she would take the onion down and wake up whoever was home in the morning by whacking them over the head with it. I pitied poor Captain Crenshaw, and if Viggo were wise, he would find somewhere else to ring in the new year.

Pulling in the parking lot of Aunt Tasoula's salon, I cut the engine to my Prius and got out for my appointment. This was Nik's and my first New Year's Eve together, and I wanted to look extra special. The problem was, when Aunt Tasoula got excited, her hands trimmed as fast as her mouth moved.

I stepped around the hairy mossy pebble she had left outside the door to her shop. On New Year's Day, whoever stepped on the stone when entering her shop would have good luck all year long. I had to admit it was a brilliant way to draw more customers inside, but all I could think of was having other people's germs on my feet.

Not to mention, I wasn't letting anything hairy or mossy touch any part of me.

Since Ma had claimed the goddess of love and beauty, Aphrodite, for her restaurant name first, Aunt Tasoula had chosen the queen of the gods, Hera, for her hair salon, Hera's Halo. I pulled out a sterile wipe and ran it over the last free seat three times before I sat down to wait for my turn.

I glanced at a magazine of celebrity gossip news on the table and wrinkled my nose, imagining the germs that must be covering the pages. Pulling out a clean copy of my own gardening magazine, I thumbed through it before scanning the room. The salon chairs looked like gold thrones, the capes like a queen's robe, and even the hair dryers were painted like crowns with precious gems adorning them. My aunt kept a sterilized pink cape that no one else used in the back just for me.

The waiting room was full, with the people who came in after me swinging on the swing in one corner and twirling on the stripper pole in the other corner. My aunt was a firm believer in multi-tasking, combining exercise and entertainment was just one example.

"I'm so excited to be here," the woman beside me said. She had short, light brown hair styled chicly, small fashionable spectacles perched on her nose, and dressed just as smartly in a soft sweater, slacks, and shoe boots.

"Are you new to town?" I asked with a smile.

"Pardon my manners. I'm Sherry Harper." She held out her hand. "We're just in town for the weekend."

I shook her hand quickly, feeling her excitement and positive energy, then discreetly rubbed my hands on my skirt until I could excuse myself and clean them more thoroughly with my hand sanitizer. "Hi, Sherry, my name is Kalli Ballas. This is my aunt's salon."

"My husband, Bennett, booked me a massage."

"Well, he sounds like a keeper." I smiled.

"Oh, he is, but I'm onto him. He mostly booked it so he could sneak off and play Scrabble." She laughed. "Works for me. I love the spa."

"Then that's a win. My pop and papou play Scrabble."

"Pa-who?"

"Papou," I clarified. "My grandfather. They're very welcoming to newcomers. I'm sure your husband will have a great time."

"It's our fifteenth wedding anniversary. We're from the city. Bennett thought it would be nice to get away. Your town is so quaint. We've heard wonderful things about the annual New Year's Eve party."

"The town is filled with Greeks, and for us, New Year's Eve is like a second Christmas. We have a special cake called the Vassilopita, our children go door-to-door carol singing, and even Saint Vassilis looks a lot like Saint Nicholas with a sack full of more presents as well. The children love it. Adults too."

"I can only imagine. It sounds delightful. We don't have any children, but we have each other. So far, everything has been wonderful in Clearview. We even ate at this fabulous restaurant called Aphrodite's. Have you ever tried it?"

I almost snorted out loud. "That's my family's restaurant. My ma will be thrilled to hear you liked it."

"Your ma?" She eyed me with curiosity. "But the owners are Greek." Her face paled. "I'm sorry, that was rude of me."

"It's quite all right. I'm adopted, but don't tell my

ma I said that." I gave Sherry a mock horrified expression.

"Your secret's safe with me." She winked then looked across the room as Perry the big, strong, muscular masseuse motioned for her to follow him. "Looks like it's my turn." Her eyes twinkled. "It was very nice meeting you, Kalli."

"It was nice meeting you as well," I responded as I watched her follow the masseuse into a separate room in the back of the salon.

Raised voices caught my attention.

In the nail section of the spa, two women were arguing. I squinted to get a closer look. Bessie Halifax was arguing with Delilah Doolittle. Bessie was a more voluptuous, darker blonde than Delilah. According to the rumor mill, Bessie had always wanted whatever Delilah had, and that hadn't changed one bit, even though they'd been out of high school for over ten years.

Bessie was a member of the Town Council and Delilah was a successful party planner. The new mayor, Flynn Zimmerman, had chosen Delilah to plan the New Year's Eve party at the Community Center, but Bessie had tried to sway her to choose Roman Cromwell—Delilah's competition—to plan the party.

"If you try to sabotage one more thing for tonight's party, I'm going to sue you and your evil sidekick, Roman." Delilah's face was flushed.

She was usually so calm and collected, I'd never seen her this frazzled.

"I don't know what you're talking about." Bessie inspected the nail on the hand Rosy, the nail tech, had just finished, instructing her to make the accent nail on the other hand bolder. She looked back at Delilah. "I have better things to do than worry about you." Her lips tipped up ever so slightly. "Like have coffee with Viggo when I finish here."

Delilah's face paled then flushed pink. "Wasn't it enough that you ruined my relationship with Andrew? Now you're trying to sabotage my chances with Viggo? I don't believe anything you say."

"You don't own Viggo. He's free to take whomever he wants to the party tonight. If he'd wanted to take you, he would have asked you already." She shrugged. "I'm sure he'll ask me today. That's why I'm at the salon. Although, it's hard to look any better than I already do." Her gaze traveled up and down Delilah. "You on the other hand could use some serious help in the makeover department. You would think you would be more put together than you are right now. Better pull it together by tonight, darling."

"I've been a little busy putting out fires today, no thanks to you. For your information, Viggo asked me for coffee first, but I didn't have time for that, either. But don't you worry. I plan to make it up to him later."

"What does that mean?" Bessie narrowed her eyes.

"It means Viggo already asked me to be his date tonight, but he doesn't need you as an appetizer first when the main course is waiting."

"Looks like he's starting with dessert if you ask me," Rosy said as she pointed to the street. She was a curvy woman with rounded cheeks and snappy brown eyes. "I'd say you're both out of luck."

All eyes turned to watch Viggo Stevens and Zelda Night stroll down the sidewalk together...whatever *that* meant.

~

DESPITE ALL THE SETBACKS, Delilah pulled off the perfect New Year's Eve party with the help of the town's new maintenance man, Leonard Murphy. Clearview Community Center was rockin'. The place was decked out with all the bells and whistles in silver and gold. A knife thrower entertained volunteers in one corner while a live band played in the other corner, with a bar and buffet table in between.

Tables were scattered around the room with a large dance floor in the middle. There was even a replica of the NYC Time's Square ball hanging from the ceiling that would drop at the stroke of midnight. Finally, all the local restaurants were holding raffles for a dinner for two in the coming new year, with proceeds going to support the town.

Ma was decked out in a fancy version of her trademark polyester, with her beehive teased extra high, while Aunt Tasoula sparkled in sequins and glitter. Pop wasn't thrilled sitting at the same table as Ma's ex, Tate, but now that Aunt Tasoula was dating him, he was left with no choice but to grin and bear it. At least Chloe, Captain Crenshaw, Papou Homer, and YiaYia Dido were at the same table as them, but YiaYia was chasing a bouncing Frona more than she was sitting.

My cousins and Nik's were all in attendance. Kosmos, Winnie, Silas, and Zena shared a table, with Yanni, Eleni, and Thalia going solo. Jasper joined them when it was clear no one else was taking the last vacant seat.

"Thank the Lord this is the last official party of the holidays," Nik said to me at our table. "I can't take any more craziness."

"Winter solstice won't be over until January sixth. We still have the Goblin Games to deal with."

"No...our *families* do." He took a sip of his beer and

sighed deep. "You and I are going to hibernate in our house until spring."

"You mean houses." I raised my wineglass.

"Two homes one roof...unless you want to knock down the only wall left between us." He took my hand in his. *Just imagine what our lives could look like.*

"I am." I chuckled. "You think the holidays are crazy. Can you imagine Wolfgang and Prissy together? I don't know if we would survive that."

*We won't know unless we try.* He kissed my hand.

"Baby steps, remember?" I squeezed his hand before pulling mine away to take a big sip of chardonnay.

"Did I hear someone say baby?" Jaz's face lit up as she slid into a seat at our table, looking like a sexy siren in a slinky red silk dress.

"For the love of God, don't mention babies." Boomer sighed. "Ever since we adopted our fur babies, my lovely girlfriend has been obsessed with babies of all kinds."

"Well, if you made an honest woman out of me, we could make our own so I wouldn't have to obsess over other people's."

"Well, someone keeps ruining the surprise, so it's not exactly my fault." He held up his hands. "Call me old-fashioned, but I really want to ask you myself."

"Well, maybe you need to get with the times. In today's world, it's perfectly acceptable for a woman to propose to a man."

"And so you have...three times."

"And you never answer." She patted his cheek.

He caught and kissed her hand. "It wouldn't be very gentlemanly to say no, but not very gallant to say yes, either. Just put getting engaged out of your mind, and maybe it just might happen in the new year." He winked.

Jaz squealed and clapped her hands.

Nikos the Greek raised a brow at me as if to say I only asked to knock down a wall.

I rolled my eyes, knowing we were talking about way more than sheetrock and plaster.

A scream pierced the air, saving me from a conversation I wasn't ready to have, and the room settled to a hushed silence. All eyes traveled to the front of the room.

"What on earth is going on?" I whispered.

"Nothing good by the looks of it," Nik said in full detective mode.

Delilah's jaw hung open as a knife pinned the bun on the top of her head to the wall.

Nik's hand hovered over where his gun would usually be, but he was off duty and wasn't carrying for once. I knew he was kicking himself for that. He pursed his lips and watched closely, poised and ready to move if need be.

"Are you crazy?" Delilah sputtered, gaping at the knife thrower. "You're lucky you missed."

Scout Armstrong arched a black brow high and crossed her tattooed arms over her leather clad chest. "I don't miss."

"Then what was that?" Delilah pointed a finger at the top of her head.

"A warning."

"I have witnesses."

"I don't care." Her spiked hair looked as sharp as her knives. "The amount you paid me isn't what we negotiated."

"Prove it."

"Our deal was verbal, but you know exactly what we agreed upon."

"I paid you what I felt was fair based on your performance this evening. I have to say I'm disappointed." Delilah shrugged one slender shoulder. "Sorry."

"You *will* be." Scout glared.

Delilah gasped.

Scout looked around the room, her gaze settling on our new mayor, Flynn Zimmerman, who stood watching with Captain Crenshaw. Scout didn't say a word, just walked forward and raised her hand. Delilah flinched as Scout grabbed the knife and yanked it out of the wall. With one last glance around the room, she walked out. Everyone breathed a sigh of relief and conversations resumed, but a definite chill had settled over the room.

Something told me we had a lot more out with the old to come before we could ring in the new.

**4**

———

Viggo passed Scout on his way into the Community Center, frowned over a clearly shaken Delilah, and made his way over to her, ignoring a gloating Zelda and Knox along the way. The band began to play, and bodies filled the dance floor.

Nik held out his hand. I allowed him to lead me onto the floor and into his arms. We danced in silence, just enjoying each other as we swayed to the music. The children had all received their gifts from Saint Vasilis while the adults were engrossed in a big card playing tournament at one of the tables.

New Year's Eve was considered a lucky time, so every year a card-playing marathon was held at the bash. Ma got so mad at Pop because that was his excuse not to dance with her as he and Papou sat front and center.

Ma pouted as Aunt Tasoula twirled by like a ballerina in a music box wound too tight, cackling with every pirouette performed on Tate's arm. Ma mimicked her cackle and rolled her eyes, shooting Pop another glare.

Sherry slid into my line of sight, changing my focus as she said with a huge smile, "I won the raffle for dinner at your parents' restaurant. Isn't that so exciting?"

"Congratulations," I said.

Nik nodded to Bennett, who tilted his head in return. Bennett was a dashing man in his fifties, with salt and pepper hair that gave him a distinguished look. Sherry giggled as Bennett spun her around and waltzed her away.

"The Harpers seem nice." Nik studied the couple. "Your father says he's one heck of a Scrabble player."

"I think it's sweet that he surprised Sherry with a weekend away for their fifteenth wedding anniversary."

"That's what happens when you don't have walls between you." Nikos locked eyes with mine for an intense moment before winking at me.

"Very funny. Can we just enjoy being a couple and not put any more pressure on moving in together?"

"Sure," Nik said, his blue eyes softening as they held mine captive. *It is kind of exciting deciding your place or mine every night.*

"Exactly," I said on a laugh. "Speaking of couples, it looks like Delilah won."

Nik's brow quirked. "Won what?"

"Viggo. For the night, at least." I pointed across the room.

"I didn't realize there was a competition for him," Nik grumbled as he glanced in their direction.

"You have no idea."

"It doesn't surprise me. He likes *all* women a little too much."

"I was at my aunt's hair salon this afternoon, and

he walked by with Zelda. So much for him wanting to avoid his obsessed ex. They looked pretty chummy to me."

"Yet she's here with that other model, Knox." Nik pointed across the room to another spot.

"Except they don't look very chummy, do they?" I studied them for a moment. They were talking with their hands, and judging by the expressions on their faces, the conversation looked intense.

"No, they do not." Nik shrugged.

Viggo was comforting Delilah while her new assistant, Claudett Fox, ran around keeping everything on track. Ma told me Delilah's normal assistant, Cameron Oswald, who had helped with Ma's Christmas party, broke her leg in a ski accident. Delilah had to hire someone else from the temp agency last minute to fill in until Cameron was back on her feet.

"I can't believe Bessie Halifax is here with Delilah's ex, Andrew Ledger," I added. Andrew was a banker, with suit, tie, and slicked back hair. The complete opposite of a Viking. "Bessie and Delilah went to high school with Jaz and me. They have been enemies since forever. I guess Bessie seduced Andrew. That's why Delilah broke up with him. He has been trying to win Delilah back for a long time now. For a minute, it looked like she might give him another chance."

"What happened?"

"Your cousin Viggo showed up."

Nik grunted and then turned pensive. "Speaking of cousins." Nik nodded toward my cousin Yanni, who was talking to Senator Parker West. "You think he'll ever find someone special?"

"Well, I was hoping Delilah's sister Dixie might be

an option. Dixie just bought a new house, so Yanni said she hired him to do the landscaping in the spring. Yanni doesn't normally mix business with pleasure, so there probably goes that sliver of hope."

"I wonder what business he has with the senator?" Nik wrinkled his brow, watching the two engrossed in conversation.

"I have no clue. I didn't even know they knew each other." My cousin Yanni was in his forties. The senator looked to be around the same age. A blond-haired, blue-eyed smooth operator from what I'd heard around town. "Isn't the senator pretty new to town?"

"Yes, but I saw them talking at the gym together. And I'm pretty sure West is working with Thalia to find a house."

"Ah, that's probably it, then. I'm sure she recommended Yanni for his landscaping as well."

"You're probably right." Detective Dreamy spun me around and I giggled.

"It's almost midnight. Did you make any resolutions?"

"Well, I—"

The ball started to drop, and everyone started to count.

"Ten..."

"Nine..."

"Eight..."

"Seven..."

"Six..."

"Five..."

"Four..."

"Three..."

"Two..."

Suddenly, the room plunged into darkness.

Hours later, in the early morning, I changed into yoga pants and a soft sweatshirt. I sat at the kitchen table, sipping chardonnay. Nik had also changed into sweatpants and a sweatshirt, then met me over at my place. I handed him a beer. It had been one eventful evening.

Chaos had broken loose after the power went out.

We all fumbled around in the dark until Leonard got the generator started. When the lights came back on, Aunt Tasoula was sprawled across the floor with her tutu of a skirt flipped up over her head. Ma was under a table with her hands holding her hive in place. Fights over who won the card game ensued as cards were scattered everywhere. The food table filled with desserts had collapsed to the floor, and the champagne fountain was dry with its pyramid of glasses toppled in shattered shards.

No one had rung in the new year, and that was a bad sign.

By the time the dust settled, the ball had already dropped, and everyone had missed the moment. The mamas were positive it was the work of those naughty goblins, but I wasn't so sure. I'd had this strange vibe all evening that something was afoot. When a head count was done, Viggo and Delilah weren't there.

Delilah's temp assistant Claudett wasn't very happy with her boss.

"I'm sorry," Nik said, breaking through my thoughts.

"For what?" I looked at him funny.

"This was not the way I wanted to start the new year with you." He ran a hand over his head and down the back of his neck as if he were tense. He looked tired. I knew I was. This wasn't exactly how I envisioned this evening going, either.

"It wasn't your fault the evening turned into a total disaster." I reached out and squeezed his hand, feeling his regret even though he wasn't thinking anything.

"No, but I didn't have to pressure you into knocking down the wall between our apartments. It wasn't the best way to close out this past year."

My cat, Miss Priss, chose that moment to prance regally into the room. She looked down her nose at us, meowed her displeasure at the two of us keeping her awake, and then regally strolled out of the room once more.

I groaned. "And that is the main reason why I hesitate," I tried to explain. "Prissy doesn't play nice in the sandbox. She doesn't like to share her space with many people. She barely tolerates you. I can't imagine the kind of craziness we would have to live with if she had to deal with Wolfgang on a daily basis."

"At least we would have a lot more room for them to roam."

"Or hide."

"He would never hurt her."

"It's not her getting hurt that I'm worried about. Wolfgang is a big baby. He wouldn't stand a chance against her. She can get pretty nasty when things don't go her way. I worry poor Wolfy won't be the same if Prissy unleashes her claws."

"Trust me, Wolf can hold his own. He adores her almost as much as he adores you. He's patiently waiting for her to come around like you did."

"Patiently?" I laughed. "Mr. Wigglebutt is anything but patient."

"I think Miss Priss likes him, too. She just wants to make sure he knows she's in charge. Not unlike someone else I know. I can relate to his impatience." My Nikos winked at me.

"You're hilarious." I shot him a mock scowl.

"I try." He smirked.

"So, what do you think happened with the power tonight, anyway?" I traced the rim of my wineglass three times.

"I'm not sure. The mayor checked and no other place in town lost power. After Leonard got the generator started, he said he would look at the system later today considering it's now the middle of the night. Captain told us all to go home and get some sleep."

"Well, I'm glad you're here with me now."

"Me too. Wall or no wall, your place or mine…it doesn't really matter as long as we're together." He reached out and held my hand, and I could tell he was trying not to think any thoughts to pester or sway me.

That just made my heart melt all the more.

"I'm making a resolution right now." I looked him in the eyes. "I resolve to honestly consider moving in together."

*Yes!* He cleared his throat and let go of my hand. I mean, "Really?"

I chuckled softly. "Really."

"Happy New Year, Kalli." Nik leaned forward and gave me a kiss.

"Happy New Year, Nik. Let's hope this year starts off better than how the last year ended."

"Cheers to that." We both drank.

Suddenly, Nik's cell phone rang. We made eye contact before he answered.

"Detective Stevens here." Nik frowned. "Slow down and say that again." His eyes widened. "Sit tight. I'll be right there." He hung up and stood.

"Who was that?"

Our eyes met. "Viggo."

"What happened?" I stood, too.

Nik closed his eyes for a moment, then opened them while shaking his head. "Delilah Doolittle is dead, and my cousin Viggo is with her."

So much for a happy new year.

**5**

———————

"Start from the beginning and tell me everything. Don't leave any detail out. You never know what might be important to figuring out what exactly happened," Nik said to Viggo while we sat in his patrol car out front of Dixie Doolittle's house.

The crime scene had been taped off, with various forms of first responders, law enforcement officers, CSI, and the new medical examiner, Clint Davis. Lights were flashing everywhere in the dark sky. The sun hadn't quite risen yet, but soon Clearview would awake to the news that a murder had happened to one of their own.

Nik had called 911 as soon as he hung up with Viggo, and then we had both jumped into his police car. I wasn't a police officer, but I'd convinced Nik to let me tag along for moral support since Viggo was his cousin, and I was Nik's official girlfriend. Family was family, and I intended to be there for my man.

Whether he liked it or not.

"I had a little too much to drink." Viggo stared at his lap with a furrowed brow, his shaking hands fiddling with the bottom of his sherpa coat. He ran the back of one hand over his sweating forehead, even though the January temps were below freezing, then he looked up at Nik with confused, troubled eyes.

"It's okay, Viggo," I interjected, looking over the back of the passenger side front seat. "We're here to help you." Now that he was under suspicion for murder, there was no riding shotgun for him.

Nik's gaze sliced over to me briefly and then back to his cousin. I couldn't tell if that meant *thank you* or *butt out*. This whole supportive girlfriend thing was new to me.

Viggo inhaled a deep breath. "I was still comforting Delilah over the whole incident with that knife thrower, Scout. And then Delilah's ex, Andrew, showed up with Bessie, her rival from high school, knowing it would bother Delilah to see them together since Bessie is the woman he had an affair with. Delilah was a mess, and I felt bad for her."

"Did you tamper with the electrical system?" Nik watched his cousin closely.

Viggo's eyes widened. "No, why would I do that?"

"I don't know why you do half the things you do, cuz." Nik rubbed his temples before continuing. "The power went out right before midnight. Everyone missed seeing the new year come in. By the time Leonard got the generator back on, the place was a disaster, and several people were injured."

"We weren't even there. I couldn't take much more of the Zelda and Knox show and was ready to leave myself. So, I convinced Delilah's temp assistant, Claudett, to handle the rest of the evening because Delilah wasn't feeling well. The woman didn't look very happy about it, but I didn't give her much choice. We left, and I took Delilah home."

"I didn't see her car still at the Community Center.

Tell me you didn't drive after you admitted you had too much to drink?" Nik frowned. "Doesn't Delilah live in the apartments right down from the Community Center? You could have walked."

"She told Claudett to load the rest of the supplies after the party in her car and drive it to her own apartment. Delilah planned to pick up her car from Claudett the next day. Delilah wasn't staying at her apartment. Her sister, Dixie, was out of town for the holiday and asked her to house sit. We took a cab." Viggo let out a huff. "I'm not stupid, cuz."

"That remains to be seen." Nik grunted. "Continue."

"I made sure she got home okay, and she asked me to come in for a nightcap. We rang in the new year together, and I passed out in her sister's bed."

"Of course, you did." Nik's face looked flushed, and waves of anger radiated off of him as a muscle in his jaw bulged.

I had a feeling this line of questioning had something to do with whatever had happened between them in the past.

"I didn't do anything wrong," Viggo hissed, scowling at his cousin. "Delilah and I were both single, no matter what crazy Zelda or obsessed Andrew might think."

"What happened next," I asked, trying to refocus the questioning while attempting to diffuse the situation.

Viggo took a moment to regain his composure, then looked at me instead of Nik. "Sometime later, I heard a noise downstairs. It woke me up, but when I looked beside me, Delilah was gone." He held up his hands, looking lost, helpless...and innocent.

Either he really was innocent, or he was one heck of an actor.

He went on. "I assumed she went down for a drink of water or something, so I fell back to sleep while waiting for her to come back up. When I woke up the second time, she still wasn't there."

Nik started to look less frustrated and more concerned. He wrote something in his notes and then looked up at his cousin. "What did you do next?"

"I hollered out to her. When she didn't answer, I went down to find her." Viggo's eyes filled with genuine sorrow and regret. "I never thought I would find her stabbed to death with a kitchen knife sticking out of her chest. It was horrible. I can't believe she's dead." He stared off and a dazed expression settled over his face. "I've never seen a dead body before. It's not something I ever want to see again."

"It *is* horrible and not something that is easily forgotten. I know from experience." I shivered. "I'm sorry you had to witness that."

Viggo swallowed hard and just nodded, looking vulnerable and less like a big strong Viking at the moment.

Nik flipped through his notebook and concentrated. "The door was open, but it doesn't look like it was broken into, yet a few drawers were overturned, indicative of a burglary attempt. We won't know if anything was taken until Dixie returns and does inventory."

"What do you think happened?" I asked.

"Either the burglar broke in and Delilah caught him in the act, so he killed her. Or someone with a vendetta against Delilah followed her and killed her, then tried to stage a burglary. We'll know more after her sister returns. But I do know one thing. That was a kill strike. That knife was precisely placed to kill with one stab by someone who knew how to use one."

"Oh, God, I own a knife," Viggo blurted.

Nik's eyes widened. "I thought you were a lover not a fighter. Why on earth do you have a knife?"

"Protection. I don't like guns."

"Yes, because models are so scary," Nik responded dryly.

Viggo's voice held an edge to it. "You have no idea how ruthless the modeling business can be."

I quirked a brow.

Nik narrowed his eyes.

"Just because you're from another country doesn't mean you can do whatever you want. We do have laws here, cousin." Nik rubbed his forehead. "What kind of knife do you even have?"

Viggo shrugged. "A Ka-Bar knife."

Nik gaped. "That knife has a seven-inch blade."

"So? I'm a big guy. I need a big knife."

"You're not Crocodile Dundee, for Zeus's sake." Nik slapped his hand down on his notebook. "No one needs a knife that big for their personal protection. And in Connecticut, it's illegal to carry a knife with a blade longer than four inches."

"Oh, I didn't know." A worried expression crossed Viggo's features. "What does that mean?"

Nik shook his head and looked at me as if he didn't have the energy to even form the words.

"How do I put this...?" I bit my bottom lip and struggled for ways to sugar coat it, but there was no denying the truth. I folded my hands together and looked Viggo in the eye as I stated the facts in true Nikos fashion. "It means your stupidity level just went up a notch, and your future's not looking so bright."

By the expression on my favorite detective's face, I'd provided the perfect explanation.

~

A FEW HOURS later on New Year's Day, Ma picked up Aunt Tasoula, Chloe, and me. We each emptied all the water jugs in our houses and places of business and loaded them in Aphrodite's catering van.

Pop put the last of the restaurant's jugs in the van and closed the door.

"Thank you, Amos. You a good man." Ma kissed his cheek, then frowned. "Why you wear two different shoes?"

"Because someone stole the match to both." He shook his head. "Now my two favorite pairs of shoes are ruined. Why someone do this to me?" He talked with his hands flailing about. "What I do to anyone?"

"You look foolish." Ma swiped her hand through the air. "Go change."

"Into what? Those my favorite shoes."

"I say good riddance. They both old and smelly."

"I old and smelly." He patted his chest and frowned. "What you do? You say good riddance to me, too?"

Ma thought about that for a minute and then shrugged. "Maybe, if you no go change. I bought you brand new, no-slip kitchen shoes just the other day."

"But Ophelia..." He whined. "I no like them. They too new and stiff."

"But they no smell." She pointed her finger in his face. "Go break them in before you fall and break your stubborn neck."

Pop threw his hands up and grumbled every mismatched step of the way back into the kitchen, mumbling a string of Greek I didn't want to interpret.

"That man drive me crazy." Ma opened the driver's side door to the big van. "Who in Mount Olympus would want his smelly old shoes?"

Aunt Tasoula shrugged, hopping in the passenger side. "Let's go, ladies. No time to worry about smelly, mismatched shoes. We need these jugs refilled with Saint Vassilis's water and blessed by Father Papadopoulos as soon as possible. Chop, chop." She clapped her hands. "I have full day at salon. Everyone want a makeover in the new year." Aunt Tasoula patted her own hair. "I no help it they all want to look like me."

Ma grunted, earning a sharp look from her sister, then she went into a choking fit.

"See?" Aunt Tasoula waggled her finger with a smug look. "I *extra* protected this year. You make fun at me, and the karmama get you. Remember when Ramona back in high school grunt at me? The karmama got her, too. She have voice like tuba ever since. I call her Ratuba now." Aunt Tasoula nodded her head once.

Ma rolled her eyes.

The Renewal of Waters took place on New Year's Day to keep evil spirits away from people's homes and places of business. Nik's family and mine took the tradition seriously and went one step further by giving offerings to water nymphs known as Naiads.

They were just as positive that these creatures existed as they were positive the goblins were still up to no good. The antics they went to in order to stop them were ridiculous, but there was no arguing with Greek mamas.

I simply went along to get along, or I would never

hear the end of it. Chloe handed me her crutches and I stored them in the van then helped her into the back seat while I slid into the other side.

"I, for one, am all for this blessing," Chloe said. "Oh, woe is me. My poor nephew, Viggo, needs all the help he can get. If only he stay home last night like a good boy, I would have whacked him over the head with my big onion." She tsked. "That boy has always been cursed with bad luck. I fear this is very bad year for him."

"Don't worry, Chloe. Nik will figure out what happened," I said, hoping I was right. Something was definitely going on with Viggo, but I was fairly certain he wasn't a killer.

"I hope you right, dear." Chloe's perfectly-put-together chic appearance looked a little wrinkled today. "I know Viggo is his blood, but I worry my Nikos won't fight so hard for *this* family member."

"Why is that?" I held my breath, waiting for some insight, finally.

Nik had been very closed mouthed about that whole side of his family, yet he wanted me to knock down a wall between us. I wasn't going to knock down a physical wall if he wasn't willing to knock down his emotional one.

"Honestly, I really don't know." She folded her hands together in her lap and looked off as if remembering. "They used to be so close, then one day they weren't. I asked him about it years ago, but he no say why."

Well, that didn't help at all, and now I was more curious than ever.

We pulled into the parking lot of our Greek Orthodox Church, with Ma weaving between all the parked cars and pulling the van right up to the curb in front of the door like she owned the place. She cut the engine and hopped out, bypassing the line of people, and tapping a couple of strapping young men on their shoulders.

"Come along, boys. Put those muscles to good use." Ma took a couple steps toward our van then stopped in her tracks to glare at them over her shoulder. "Don't tell me you no hear me." She pointed her finger at them. "Don't make me call your mamas."

The boys came running.

They were all related to us in some way. Those who weren't, were related to Nik's family, so all the mamas knew each other. They weren't kidding when they said it took a village to parent. Our families *were* a village, and they all parented together.

A Greek mama was *not* someone you wanted to make mad.

"Ophelia Ballas, as patient as ever I see." Father Papadopoulos came to a stop before Ma, holding a Bible in front of him.

"It's my bad back, Father." Ma slumped and suddenly looked helpless and feeble rather than like Athena the goddess of wisdom and war which she had embodied only moments ago. "I fell when the lights went out at the party," she continued in a whine that was very similar to Pop's. "I no can wait in line today."

"I do believe you're not the only one who was hurt last night." He eyed her suspiciously. "Yet I don't see anyone else cutting the line."

"Oh, woe is me." She placed the back of her hand on her forehead. "It's Mantrakoukos, I tell you. That ugly, short legged, stocky chief goblin hides all day long, but the minute the lights go out, he tease me all night long. I get *no* sleep."

"It's true." Aunt Tasoula nodded gravely. "My sister

suffers. She has the inzombia." Aunt Tasoula made the sign of the cross. "Is scary."

Ma swayed dramatically.

Father Papadopoulos grabbed her arm to steady her.

I tried hard not to roll my eyes.

"I even burned the log. It no work. Now my poor Amos has no stinky shoes. Help me, Father, please," Ma wailed. "I need this water blessed now."

"Of course, of course. Right this way." Father hustled off with his Bible open, already chanting a prayer, and came to a stop where the boys had carried the many jugs and refilled the water.

My birth father, Father Michael Conery, and my half-brother, Jasper, were both volunteering by assisting Father Papadopoulos. They both waved at me and smiled.

They looked more like they could be father and son rather than Michael and me were father and daughter, with their dark wavy hair. Michael had hazel eyes, where Jasper's were the same green as my birth mother, Ruby's, and my own.

I waved back as I watched them work. Jasper was hands-on, while Michael was happy to direct others and keep his hands in his pockets.

I might be a mini replica of Ruby Winehouse, but my quirks were all my birth father, Michael Conery's. I wasn't anything at all like Ruby, and I already had a father. I didn't need two, and he wasn't interested in filling that role. But it was nice getting to know him as a person. He wasn't at all like I had expected him to be, and it was nice to finally have someone who could relate to what it was like to be me.

Ma stood up straight and dusted off her hands, signaling for the boys to carry the jugs back to the car right away. "What?" she asked when she saw my arched eyebrow. "If you have something to say to me, Kalliope Ballas, I suggest you say it now."

"Trust me, I have no words," I said, meaning it. Sometimes my ma amazed me at the lengths she would go to get what she wanted.

"Smart girl." Ma winked and hopped back into the van with no shame whatsoever, and an equally shameless Aunt Tasoula as her sidekick.

I helped Chloe back into the van without another word, ready for this day to be over with, and it had barely begun. We arrived at Hera's Halo with thick black smoke pouring out of her chimney.

"Soula, I think your shop is on fire." Ma threw the van into park and ran out quite easily for someone with so-called back problems.

"Oh, no." Chloe wobbled out of the van, and I handed her crutches to her.

"Wait!" Aunt Tasoula yelled, trying to beat my ma inside, but Ma was too quick when she was on a mission.

By the time Chloe and I made our way through the front door, we all had our hands plugging our noses. The fireplace flames burned an unsightly color as smelly dark smoke funneled up the chimney.

Ma's jaw fell open. "Soula, you didn't!"

Aunt Tasoula raised her chin a notch. "Oh, please, you know you want to thank me for it."

"So *that's* the extra protection you were talking about," Chloe said, her eyes dawning with under-standing.

I vaguely remembered from my childhood someone telling me that in order to protect your house or place of business from naughty goblins, you had to burn a smelly shoe in the fireplace. The foul smell would keep the goblins away for days. But so much for a full day at the salon. The smell was keeping everyone else away, too.

My eyes widened as a thought occurred to me...

I suddenly knew what had happened to my pop's shoes.

"Where are you headed now?" Jaz asked later that day when I came down from my loft at Full Disclosure with my coat and tote bag slung over my arm while I scrubbed my hands with hand sanitizer.

"I feel so bad for Dixie Doolittle," I said. "Can you imagine coming home and finding out your twin sister is dead, while housesitting your house, no less?"

"No." Jaz gave me a horrified look. "You're not my twin, but you might as well be. I couldn't imagine losing you. I literally wouldn't be able to live without you. Love you by the way."

"Exactly. Me either, sister. Love you, too." I put my coat on and adjusted the items in my tote bag. "Ma gave me some Mosaiko to take to her, so I think I'll take my lunch break now if that's okay."

"You might work out of my place, but you're your own boss. And now that your lingerie line is doing so well and you're paying me rent, which *you* insisted on, you're free to do whatever you want to."

"It's only right that I pay you rent. It makes me feel better, just like paying rent for my half of your house makes me feel better, too." I pulled my gloves out of my bag and slipped them on.

"If you and Detective Dreamy bought my house and knocked down that wall, you wouldn't have to pay me anything." She winked.

"Don't you start, too," I warned her as I pulled the belt on my coat tighter. "I have a hard enough time convincing Nik that it's fun and keeps the romance alive by spending the night at each other's houses."

"Except we both know you're just afraid of change." She walked with me to the front door.

"Hey, I agreed to being official." I stopped and turned to her. "That should count for something, shouldn't it?"

"I'm sure it does," Jaz said gently and squeezed my shoulder once.

"Besides, I did make him a resolution that I would think about knocking down that wall and moving in together this year. But for now, we can't think of anything except clearing his cousin's name."

"So, Viggo is the prime suspect?" She folded another article of clothing and set it on a rack in the front window display, studying me.

"Well, he *was* in the house with her when she died." I frowned.

Her eyes widened. "Do you believe he's guilty?"

"Well, the fact that he didn't wake up when she was stabbed to death doesn't look too good for his case. He says he had too much to drink, but honestly, he seemed fine when I saw him at the party. He's a big guy. It would take a lot to make him so drunk he wouldn't wake up to sounds of a struggle. Someone getting murdered isn't exactly quiet."

"Oh, no. Poor Nik."

"I know. They might have issues, but he's still his

family. I don't know his cousin well. I would like to think anyone related to Nik wouldn't be capable of murder, but what do I know? What I *do* know is that something seems off with him."

Jaz looked around the nearly empty shop and lowered her voice. "Have you tried reading his mind?"

"I've only been around him when Nik was with me. I don't know what went on between them in the past, but I do know Nik is jealous of him. It wouldn't go over well if he saw me touching Viggo, no matter how innocent it might be."

"That's interesting. Nik doesn't seem like the jealous type."

"He's not normally, but he's different around his cousin."

"Hmmm, well maybe you'll run into Viggo alone sometime."

"Maybe, but for now, I'm going to walk to Dixie's antique shop." I peeked out the window at the sunny sky.

"You really think she went to work today?"

"Nik said he talked to her at the station this morning. She said the night of the murder, she was gone antiquing in the city, spent the night, and came back today to find her sister dead. Her house is a crime scene, and Delilah's apartment is also off limits during the investigation. Dixie has an apartment above her shop that she had planned to rent out now that she bought a new house. I guess she's going to stay there for the time being until the investigation is over with."

"That makes sense." Jaz wrinkled her brow. "I don't know Dixie that well, but give her my best and let her know, as a small business owner, I'm there for her. If she needs anything, I'm happy to help."

"I will." I waved and headed out the door.

Tightening my coat against the January chill in the air, I placed my tote bag in the back seat of my car, grabbed my purse and the Mosaiko, locked the car, and then headed down the street. The wind picked up, and I shivered, regretting not driving even though her shop wasn't very far. Window shoppers and dog walkers lined both sides of the streets since the sun was shining on this first day of the new year. Many people were off and eager to start their resolutions.

So why did I feel a nagging sensation in the pit of my gut?

Right as I got to Doolittle's Doodads, I had the strongest sensation that I was being watched. I knew the feeling as I had felt this before, when other murders had happened and people were after me. But I didn't have anything to do with this murder other than dating the accused's cousin.

I slowly turned around in a circle but didn't see anything unusual. And with so many people milling about, it was difficult to notice if anything was out of the ordinary. Adjusting the tray in my hands, I turned back around and entered the shop.

It hit me just how much Dixie looked like Delilah.

The difference was Delilah was sophisticated, where Dixie was artsy. Still, the resemblance was uncanny. If they wore the same outfit, you wouldn't be able to tell them apart.

Glancing around, I took in the store. The most unique looking antiques filled every nook and cranny. Jaz would love this shop. I couldn't believe we hadn't been here before. But Delilah had moved to town first about two years ago, and Dixie had only just moved here about one year ago. Life had been crazy busy with my work, new ability, and even newer boyfriend.

Shopping for myself had been the last thing on my list.

No one was in the shop at the moment, so I approached the checkout counter.

Dixie looked up and smiled. "Hi there. Welcome to Doolittle's Doodads. May I help you with something?"

"Actually, I'm here to offer you something instead."

She eyed the dish in my hand with a raised brow. "What's the catch?"

I was kind of taken aback. First of all, she didn't seem upset like someone whose twin sister had just been murdered. Second, she was awfully cynical. I hadn't been expecting that. Delilah had been all sunny smiles and bubbly personality.

"No catch," I said with a sympathetic smile. "I'm Kalli Ballas. My parents own Aphrodite's restaurant. Your sister planned our annual holiday party recently. My ma baked some dessert for you." I set the Greek chocolate biscuits on the counter.

"Oh. I don't really like desserts, but thank you." She stared at the dish.

"No problem. Maybe your customers will like some. We're just trying to help. Your sister was such a sweet woman. We're all so sorry for your loss."

Dixie nodded once, looking down at the counter.

"I've never been in your shop before." I looked around. "It's lovely."

Her lips turned down. "I love antiques, but apparently, the people in this town don't. Delilah and I only had each other. I thought I could make a living here, but so far, things aren't going that well." She let out a big breath.

"I'm sorry to hear that."

"It is what it is. That's why I went to the city over the holiday. Delilah wanted me to attend her party and wasn't happy when I told her no. I had a lead on more antiques I wanted to buy. We had an argument before I left, and I never got to say I was sorry." Dixie looked me in the eye. "I regret that."

"That has to be difficult for you."

"Delilah was always one for a good time. I've always had to struggle. She never really understood why I was so much more serious than her." Dixie shook her head. "Don't get me wrong. I loved my sister, but we never really saw eye-to-eye."

"That's a shame." I glanced at the stairs behind her. "I'm sorry you have to stay in your old apartment. You just bought a new house, right?"

She stared at me, and her face stiffened. "I know what you're thinking. If my shop isn't doing well, then how could I afford a new house?"

I didn't say a word, I just waited patiently for her to continue.

She tapped the counter. "I thought I was going to make a big sale from an antique I bought, but it turns out it wasn't worth much. I also planned to rent my apartment, so the money from that and from my shop would be enough to pay my mortgage. Now, I'm not really sure what I'll do."

"I'm sorry, Dixie. I really am."

"Are you?" She studied me. "I know who you are. You're Detective Steven's girlfriend. I also know his cousin is the number one suspect in my sister's murder."

"That's true, but that's honestly not why I came here today. I really did want to offer my sympathy and let you know there are many other small business owners in town who would love to help. All you have to do is ask. Clearview looks out for their own."

"Well, I'm used to being alone and looking after myself."

The bell over her front door chimed, and in walked Bennett Harper, looking dapper in his black wool peacoat and matching black wool peaked cap. He blinked when he saw me, then smiled wide. "Ms. Ballas, so nice to see you this fine day."

I smiled back. "Likewise, and please, call me Kalli." I slid my palms down into my pockets in hopes he wouldn't try to shake my hand.

"Then you must call me Bennett." He tipped his hat.

"Where's Sherry?" I asked, looking behind him. I really liked his wife and hoped the murder didn't ruin their anniversary weekend.

His face grew grave. "She was a bit shaken up this morning after we heard the dreadful news. I sent her off to your aunt's salon to be pampered."

I hoped Pop's smelly shoes had finished burning.

Bennett lowered his voice conspiratorially. "I told her I was off to play Scrabble with your father and grandfather, but really, I'm buying an anniversary present for her. We're having the dinner we won at your parents' restaurant tonight, so I want to surprise her with..." he looked around the store and his eyes lit up "...something like that." He pointed to an antique jewelry box. "She would love that."

"I can help you with that," Dixie said.

Bennett looked up as if just noticing her and sucked in a startled breath, his mouth falling open as he stared silently.

"Yes, sir, the murder victim was my sister. We're twins," she said wearily as if she knew she was going to get this reaction all day long. "If you don't mind, I'd like to stick to business. About the jewelry box. Would you like me to wrap that for you?"

He snapped his gaping mouth closed. "I'm so sorry for your loss, ma'am." He cleared his throat, looking embarrassed. "Yes, please. Whatever it costs, I'll take it. I spare no expense when it comes to my Sherry."

"I'll see you later," I interjected. "Have a nice time at dinner." I waved to Bennett and gave Dixie a parting smile.

She didn't smile back.

I let myself out the door where the frigid temperature outside was warmer than within.

AFTER I GOT BACK to Full Disclosure, I didn't go inside to do more work on my spring collection. Instead, I hopped in my Prius and drove to Yanni's landscaping business. The weather had taken a sudden turn for the worse and it was snowing steadily now, when the forecast hadn't called for any precipitation.

As confusing as my conversation with Dixie Doolittle had been.

Pulling into the parking lot of Yanni's Yards, I cut the engine and went inside. The building Yanni leased wasn't overly large. It mostly consisted of a small sitting area with a reception desk, his office, and a planning room with a large table and chairs. Out back, he had a greenhouse filled with plants, shrubs, trees, and flowers he nurtured all winter long. An outdoor garden that was dormant now would be blooming come spring and vibrant by summer.

The door buzzed as I entered the empty lobby, but moments later, Yanni walked out of his office with a cup of coffee in his hand.

He had a thick head of dark curly hair, thick eyebrows over rich brown eyes, and a thick five o'clock shadow, even after shaving twice a day. He raised a brow and one corner of his lips tipped up just a hair when he saw me.

He nodded once. "Hey, Kalli. What brings you here?" He took a sip of his steaming coffee and gestured to one of the seats in the waiting room. "I'd offer you coffee, but I know you're not into caffeine, and, no, I don't have any herbal tea." He gestured to the water cooler in the corner. "Water?"

"Sure." I waited as he poured me a glass then handed it to me.

"Thank you." I took a sip as I sat on a sofa across from an overstuffed chair where he sat. "I see your receptionist desk is empty. What happened to Sadie?"

His face grew pinched. "She didn't work out."

"Ah, and that had nothing to do with you?"

He shrugged. "I have high standards."

"Mmmm," was all I said.

Yanni was a great guy, but he could be difficult, at best. He was a perfectionist. He had a crew to help him with doing the landscaping, but he couldn't seem to keep any office assistant, man or woman. He would need to figure something out come spring because his business had really taken off.

"Can I help you with something, cousin? I'm a one man show and a little busy at the moment."

"Are you mapping out plans for new clients?" I asked curiously, studying him closely. "I saw you talking to Dixie Doolittle at Diner Delights last week. I thought maybe you were on a date at first."

He let out a snort. "Definitely not, so don't even try to meddle like the mamas. I knew there had to a reason you just randomly stopped in to see me."

"Hey, you're my favorite cousin. Don't you know that?"

"Something tells me you say that to all of us."

I winked and pleaded the fifth, then thought about his words and frowned. "Trust me, I won't try to meddle this time. I'm *glad* you weren't on a date."

He raised a thick eyebrow. "Now those are words I never expected to hear coming out of your mouth. You and all the other cousins are constantly trying to set me up. Why not now? What's the deal?"

"I don't trust her," I said, plain and simple.

"Why? I don't need a troublesome client." He narrowed his eyes. "She seemed fine to me. All business, just how I like it."

"That's the point." I finished my water and set the cup down—on a coaster, of course—turning it three times before letting go as I pondered the curious case of Dixie Doolittle. "I find it odd and a little disturbing that she seems to care more about her business than her sister being murdered."

Yanni sipped his coffee, studying me for a minute. "People grieve in different ways." He stared down into the contents of his coffee as he swirled the black liquid. "Maybe she's just suppressing how she feels."

Yanni had loved once, years ago, when he was young. He'd met Amy in college. She was a botanist, and he was a business major studying how to successfully start his own business. At the time, he wasn't sure what that was going to be.

I remembered they had been pretty serious, and had even talked marriage, but then she died tragically in a mudslide while studying abroad. He'd never gotten over losing her. He graduated college, opened a landscaping business in her honor, and threw himself into his work without ever looking back.

*That* was why the girl cousins all meddled.

"I understand people grieve differently," I said softly, "but this situation seems different. I just came from Dixie's shop. I brought her Ma's Mosaiko."

"That was nice."

"That's what I thought. Dixie, not so much. She wasn't fazed by the gesture. She seemed indifferent, saying she didn't really like desserts."

His eyes widened. "Who doesn't like Aunt Ophelia's Mosaiko?"

"Right?" I held up my hands, palms up, before continuing. "She is Delilah's *twin*. That's even closer than sisters, yet she didn't shed a tear the whole time I was there."

"That doesn't necessarily mean anything."

"I get that, but she also talked negatively about Delilah. Like they were two very different people, and her sister never understood her. She seemed bitter. She said her sister was successful and all about the party. Where according to Dixie, she has always had to work hard to get anything she wanted, yet her business is struggling. I don't get it."

"Don't get what?"

"How can she afford a new house and landscaping if her business is struggling? It doesn't add up."

Yanni blew out a large breath and scrubbed a hand over his head. "Well, I hope there's an explanation, because I've already drawn up plans for her house for this spring. She even picked out a tree that I'm holding for her in my greenhouse. I don't want to put her on the schedule and waste any more time on this if she can't afford it."

"She told me she had been counting on the sale of an antique she'd acquired, but it turned out not to be worth what she thought it was. She also planned to rent out the apartment above her shop to help pay her mortgage. I'm not sure what she'll do now that she has to live there for the time being."

I pulled out my notebook, checking over the case notes I'd been acquiring, suddenly realizing I was turning into my boyfriend. Good Lord, we were barely official, and here I was acting like an old married couple. Clearing my throat, I put my notebook back in my purse and focused.

"Did Dixie say anything out of the ordinary when she talked to you?"

"Like what?"

"I don't know." I shrugged. "Anything about her sister? Or about maybe someone being after her? After all, the murder took place in her new house. It looked like a staged robbery, yet Dixie told Detective Stevens that nothing was missing from her house. Nik says either someone was after Delilah and staged a robbery, or someone was after Dixie and mistook the two women since they look so much alike."

Yanni stared at the ceiling, deep in thought before looking back at me. "I can't think of anything that might help solve her sister's murder case. We mostly talked business. Things like what she wanted for her yard, and the type of tree she wanted. I took her into the greenhouse to pick one out, but she couldn't make up her mind. I offered to reschedule, but she was adamant she needed to pick it out that day because she had plans in the city for the weekend. I took a phone call and when I came back, she pointed to the tree she had picked, I tagged it, and then we left."

"Did she say what her plans in the city were?"

"No, just that she needed to get out of Clearview asap."

"Hmmm, she told me she had a lead on more antiques she wanted to buy, so she left for the city, and Delilah was mad that she didn't stay to attend her party."

"It makes me wonder did she really have a lead or was she just running away from her problems?" he asked.

"And that is the million-dollar question."

## 7

The next day Nik and I woke up to over a foot of snow. After the roads were clear, we both went to work in more ways than one, he just didn't know it yet. That evening we went to Rosalita's Place for dinner. I went to high school with Rosalita, and her restaurant was one of the few places I could go where I trusted her kitchen was up to my standards of clean. I still brought my own utensils, of course.

It didn't even phase Nik anymore. He was so used to my quirks.

Rosalita's was a southwestern themed Mexican restaurant. Since both of our families had businesses all over town, we liked to go to Rosalita's place on the outskirts of Clearview once in a while. Although, lately, we'd been seeing more and more people we knew.

Case in point. Parker West was sitting at a table with Nik's cousin, Thalia. Nik had said she was helping the senator find a house, but they looked pretty chummy to me. Not to mention, Bessie Halifax was sitting at another table with Andrew Ledger, Delilah's ex, even though Andrew had said their affair was over.

Bessie was head of the Town Council, and Andrew worked at the bank. Maybe it had something to do with that. Bessie covered Andrew's hand with her own. Was she comforting him over losing Delilah? Or was something more going on between them?

"Where'd you go just now?" Nik asked, snapping me from my thoughts. "You look like you're a million miles away."

"Sorry. I was just speculating on possible suspects who had a reason to want Delilah dead."

Nik glanced over his shoulder. "Ah, West. There's something about the guy I don't trust. I'm worried Thalia will fall for him, and he'll end up hurting her. As for Delilah, I can't imagine what reason he would have for wanting her dead. His whole campaign is built on cracking down on crime. That's why he moved here, apparently."

"We've certainly had our share of crime lately. Maybe he's not so bad."

Nik shrugged. "Yanni seems to like him, and your cousin doesn't like many people. They've become bros at the gym."

"Speaking of Yanni, I went to see him yesterday. He said Dixie was just a client of his, but that she was excited about his plans for her yard. She even picked out a tree in his greenhouse that he's holding for her."

"Did she say anything else?"

"She told me that she had a lead on some valuable antiques, so that's why she went to the city instead of her sister's New Year's Eve party. But Yanni said she told him she needed to get out of Clearview asap. She didn't say why," my gaze locked onto Nik's, "but she also didn't say anything about antiquing."

"You went to see Dixie? Why?" He might be asking

the question, but he already knew the answer. He knew me well.

"I've been meaning to check out her shop for a while now." I inspected my water glass before taking a sip. Then I took a bite of my taco salad.

"Look, I know you want to help me clear my cousin's name, but you're not interfering with my investigation, are you?"

"Of course not." I smiled a little too wide. "Ma made her some Mosaiko. That's all. I simply asked a few questions while I was there. She didn't seem too upset for someone who just lost their twin sister."

"Right." He studied me for a minute. "And you just had to see Yanni that day. Why?" He took a bite of his sizzling chicken fajitas.

"Do I need a reason to drop in on my cousin?"

"His shop is on the outskirts of town. You weren't exactly in the area to just drop in, and our yard is fully landscaped already. Not to mention the weather had turned for the worse. You hate driving in bad weather." Nik leaned forward until my eyes met his. "You went to see him to snoop, didn't you?"

Tension filled the air between us for a beat.

"Okay, yes, but not in the way you think." I waved my hand like it was no big deal. "I was curious if he liked Dixie as more than just a friend, that's all. I worry about him, Nik. He's my family. Just like I worry about you now, too."

Good thing Detective Dreamy couldn't read *my* mind.

Nik's face lost its stiffness. "You know Yanni doesn't like you girls meddling in his love life." Nik let my reason for being there drop, whether he believed me or not.

"We all just want him to find someone who makes

him happy." That was the truth at least. "All he does is work. That's going to get lonely after a while. But enough about all that. How's Viggo?"

"Stressed, which is understandable." Nik took a drink of his Corona. "Ma said he's sweating and fidgety, going stir crazy. I asked him who he thought might have wanted to kill Delilah or set him up. He wasn't much help in narrowing down a list. He hasn't left Ma's house since yesterday morning."

"Well, at least he'll stay out of trouble that way." I took a sip of my margarita. "Hey, what about that knife thrower? Everyone heard her say, *you'll be sorry*, to Delilah right before she left the party. And she most certainly knows how to use a knife."

"Scout Armstrong. She lives in a trailer on a small plot of land on the edge of town. She claims to have gone straight there and spent the night alone. Of course, she has no security camera and no neighbor close enough to verify her whereabouts. She forgot her cell phone at the Community Center and didn't go back for it until the next day, so there's no way to ping her location."

"Do you believe her?"

"I'm not sure." He rubbed his stubbled jaw. "I know she was desperate. She didn't have any heat or electricity when I stopped by, and it *is* winter. She obviously needed that money." He strummed his fingers on the table, looking thoughtful. "Desperation makes people do crazy things."

Just then Cameron Oswald walked into the restaurant on crutches and was seated at a table for two. She was Delilah's original full-time assistant for my parents' holiday party, until she had a skiing accident and Delilah hired a temp. Now that Delilah had been murdered, the business would go to her benefactor. A few minutes later someone joined Cameron at her table, but it wasn't Claudett Fox. It was Roman Cromwell, Delilah's competition.

What on earth were they doing together?

~

THE NEW MAYOR clearly wanted to make an impression, but others were determined to be heard as well. She called a town hall meeting to update the public on what was going on. Mayor Flynn Zimmerman sat at a head table, insisting Captain Quincy Crenshaw join her. Meanwhile, Senator Parker West demanded a seat at the table with Councilmember Bessie Halifax by his side.

Chairs were lined up in rows that filled the room. Nik and I sat with Boomer and Jaz, waiting for the show to begin. It was no secret that Flynn and Parker were both new to town and determined to make a difference to aid in their own political campaigns.

They were constantly butting heads on what to do to *save* Clearview. This murder was the perfect opportunity for them to flex their political muscles to aid in their own agendas. The diehard locals felt these newcomers hadn't lived in Clearview long enough to *really* care about the town.

Leonard Murphy, the maintenance man, set a microphone in the center of the table. He had longish auburn hair pulled back in a short ponytail and small round spectacles perched on his freckled nose. Bending over to adjust the height, he gave a nod to the mayor.

"Thank you, Mr. Murphy," she said with a smile, and he gave her a thumbs-up when her voice filtered through the speakers.

"If I could have your attention, everyone." The mayor leaned forward and spoke loud enough for the microphone to pick up, then waited for a hush to settle over the room. She was tall and slim with a short, sophisticated, gray-streaked hairdo.

A hush settled over the audience.

"I know we're all a little uneasy after this latest murder. That's to be expected. This type of crime seems to be happening way too often for my liking."

"What do you plan to do about it?" someone asked.

She sat up ramrod straight, making her as tall as Captain Crenshaw. "For one, I would like to up the presence of our police force on the streets."

"We don't have enough manpower for that, Mayor," Captain interjected, already shaking his head, his salt and pepper hair not moving an inch. His steel gray eyes locked firmly on the mayor, and his no-nonsense tone expressed his frustration.

"Exactly." She shuffled the notes in front of her for dramatic effect until they were perfectly lined up, then she clipped them together before her dark blue eyes locked onto his in a standoff. "Which is why I think we need to hire more officers and add on overtime for the ones we currently have."

"With what money?" Bessie chimed in, flipping her dark blonde waves over her shoulder. "No offense, Mayor, but the town doesn't have the budget for that."

"Which is exactly why I think we need to utilize what we *do* have," Senator West said emphatically. "And that's a town that cares about each other." He paused a beat to make eye contact with the entire room, no doubt banking on his blond-haired, blue-eyed, boy-next-door Ken doll looks to charm the audience and sway them to his side.

I was with Nik. Parker was *too* smooth. What exactly was his agenda, other than "saving" Clearview from itself? I wasn't sure he could be trusted, and he definitely wasn't right for Thalia, but he was exactly the kind of man she would go for.

I chewed my lip. *What exactly are you up to, Mr. West?*

"I think we should create a neighborhood watch in each neighborhood," West continued. "And it doesn't cost anything to impose a curfew at night. If we get everyone off the streets and into their homes, they can lock their doors and watch out for each other."

Grumbles sounded throughout the room negatively about a curfew.

"Well, *something* has to be done." The senator scanned his notes and then looked out at the audience. "What the town is currently doing obviously isn't working. It's time to try something different, don't you think?"

Shrugs, nods, and mumbles of agreement swept the room.

"In the meantime, Captain Crenshaw and his detectives are making great progress on this case," Flynn said as she shot the captain a meaningful look. "I'm sure they will have this murder wrapped up in no time if we give them additional help. Right, Captain?"

The captain sighed, nodding slightly, then glanced at Nik and Boomer with a small helpless shrug.

The mayor opened the floor to questions and the conversation lasted another thirty minutes before she finally called the meeting to an end. Most people filed out, but a few stragglers remained.

Nik, Boomer, Jaz, and I joined the captain up front.

"Nothing like pressure, Cap," Nik said.

The captain tossed his hands up. "I don't know

what Zimmerman was thinking, getting the crowd stirred up like that. West wasn't any better. They need to leave my department alone and let us do our jobs." The captain stepped several feet away and signaled for Nik and Boomer to follow him.

I motioned for Jaz to stay quiet, and we stood where we could see them but pretended to be having our own conversation...then we listened in, of course. The captain already knew the gist of what had happened from hearing Viggo's account, so I was assuming he wanted a progress report. I could relate.

I was pretty sure Nik wasn't telling me everything.

"So, where are we?" Captain Crenshaw asked as I'd suspected he would.

"Well, Viggo isn't much help," Nik said. "Ma says he's paranoid and won't leave the house."

"Believe me, I know." Quincy grunted. "We haven't had a moment alone since that man came to town."

"Viggo still won't say why he bailed on the modeling shoot he was in. His agency isn't too happy with him," Nik added.

"Neither are his ex, Zelda, or that other model, Knox," Boomer said. "It's clear Zelda is obsessed with Viggo, but if the guy turned her down, why won't she leave? And what's up with Knox? He's not dating Zelda, so why is he hanging around?"

"All good questions," the captain said. "Anything else?"

"Well, there's also Mack Finley," Nik pointed out, circling a note in his book. "He's still angry over Viggo sleeping with his wife, Theresa. Revenge is a good motivator to strike back. Maybe he still feels threatened and is trying to frame Viggo for murder so he'll disappear for good."

"Yeah, but murder? That's a bit much. Do you really think Mack is capable of murder?" the captain asked.

"He does have a temper and owns many knives," Boomer said, shaking his head with a disgusted look on his face. "There are rumors he abuses, and his wife has bruises she hides. Maybe Theresa killed Delilah to get her out of the way. She might have thought Viggo was her ticket out of an awful marriage."

"That's a possibility. Crimes of passion are common in situations like abusive relationships," the captain noted. "What about Delilah? Any enemies for her other than Theresa?"

"I think it's safe to say everyone saw Scout Armstrong throw her knife through Delilah's bun," Boomer said. "Delilah lost a chunk of hair and let Scout know in no uncertain terms she wasn't happy about that."

"Scout didn't care. Delilah did her wrong. Scout's broke," Nik added. "Broke, desperate, and angry. The perfect recipe to make someone snap."

"There's also Delilah's ex, Andrew. He was angry when Viggo showed up and Delilah chose him instead." Boomer checked his notes. "And Delilah's childhood nemesis, Bessie, made it clear she would do anything to get everything Delilah had, including Andrew and Viggo. Jealousy is a pretty strong motive for murder as well."

"One other thing," Nik added. "I saw Delilah's assistant, Cameron, having dinner with Delilah's competition and rival, Roman. That doesn't add up."

"Weren't you looking into Delilah's will?" Boomer asked.

"Yeah. It turns out, when Delilah was dating Andrew, they were planning on getting married. She and her sister had a falling out because Dixie didn't trust

Andrew. Delilah cut her sister out of her life and changed her benefactor to Andrew."

"But Delilah and Andrew broke up after he cheated on her," the captain said.

"True, and Delilah and Dixie had made up. But get this," Nik said. "Delilah hadn't changed her benefactor back to Dixie yet, so Andrew still gets everything."

"Does Dixie know?" the captain asked.

"I'm not sure. Kalli stopped by to give her some Mosaiko and offer her family's condolences, but Dixie was indifferent and said she didn't care for dessert."

"Who doesn't like Ophelia Ballas's Mosaiko?" both the captain and Boomer said at the same time.

"Exactly," Nik responded. "Kalli said Dixie doesn't seem that upset by her sister's death, either. I have to say when I talked to her, she was rather indifferent as well. Distracted almost. I heard they argued New Year's Eve morning, and then she left town until the next morning. Or so she says. The hotel she claimed to stay at didn't have a record of her."

"Well, it sounds like you have a lot of leads to look into." The captain put his coat on and looked over at Chloe who was waiting for him.

"We're on it." Boomer closed his notebook and slipped it inside his brown leather bomber jacket.

"Good, because I can't take any more *town hall* meetings," the captain grumbled and then left to take Chloe home.

The men joined Jaz and me.

"Oh, really? That's great your winter collection is doing so well." Jaz's voice rose higher than it should.

She looked fabulous per usual in a caramel-colored sweater dress that accented her amber eyes. Her honey-colored curls bounced with her animated, over-exaggerated movements. I loved the girl for being my biggest champion. If I ever asked her to help me bury a body, she would grab a shovel and not ask questions. We had that kind of friendship.

The kind that came around only once in a lifetime.

"Isn't it?" I tried to match her peppiness as I played along while not making eye contact with Nik. I smoothed my standard chignon on the back of my head then adjusted my tailored burgundy suitcoat.

Nik crossed his arms over his sport coat, just staring at me, waiting patiently.

"You two aren't fooling anyone," Boomer chimed in, pulling his car keys out of his jean's pocket. "We know you ladies heard everything."

"It's what you do with that information that worries me." Nik dipped his head until I looked him in the eye. "Promise me you won't make me worry even more than my cousin already has?"

"I promise to do my best." I kissed his cheek and made sure he didn't see the fingers I had crossed behind my back. I would do my best, all right. My best to help clear his cousin's name so we could all get on with our lives.

I had some resolutions to ponder, after all.

**8**

The next day at around noon, Nik and I rushed to Clearview Community Hospital. I kept my hands in my coat pocket, terrified of the germs I might encounter. We walked inside and headed straight for the reception desk. The last time I was here was not that long ago, when Kosmos and I went to see his girlfriend, Winnie Wallaby, our mail carrier.

I hated hospitals, but once again, I would support the people I loved.

"I'm here to see Viggo Stevens," Nik said to the receptionist.

"Let's see. He's on floor two. You'll need to fill out this form and show your IDs, then we'll give you both a visitor's badge."

We did as she suggested, and then we took the elevator to the second floor and headed straight for the nurse's station. The second we stepped off the elevator, we were hit with cold air and the smell of antiseptic to keep the germs to a minimum.

Again, Nik asked to see Viggo.

"Have a seat in the waiting room. Doc LaLone is in there with him now," the nurse said with the same neutral expression they always wore. I didn't blame them. No one wanted to be the bearer of bad news, and these poor, overworked nurses certainly didn't get paid enough to shoulder that responsibility.

It was just so hard to get a read on how worried we should be.

"I can't believe Viggo fell off your ma's roof. What was he thinking?" I sat down beside Nik and handed him the cup of horrible coffee I'd snagged from the vending machine. I kept hoping hospital coffee would get better, but it never did. Just one of the many reasons why I stuck to tea.

"I can," Nik responded. "And it's clear he *wasn't* thinking. Same as always." He sighed. "I have a roof rake that I do Ma's roof with, plus I pay for a plow service to do her driveway. There was no reason for Viggo to be up on her roof, shoveling off the snow."

"A fall like that could have killed him," I said.

"Exactly. We might have our differences, but he's still my family. I don't want to see anything bad happen to him."

Just then Doc LaLone walked over to the nurse's station. She pointed to us, and he headed our way in his white lab coat with a stethoscope hanging around his neck. He was in his sixties, with thick white hair and kind blue eyes. I'd been going to him since I was born, and I trusted him implicitly.

"Nice to see you, Kalli. How's your family?" he greeted me first.

"Good to see you, too, Doc. My family is well... crazy this time of year." I shrugged. "You know how it is."

"Ah, the goblins are back I take it."

"Apparently so." I laughed as I shook my head.

Doc looked at Nik. "Detective Stevens, how are you

holding up?"

"I've been better."

"I can only imagine. Your family has a lot going on at the moment."

Nik nodded, then furrowed his brow. "How bad is Viggo?"

"He's lucky to be alive. That's for sure. He has a few cracked ribs and a broken arm, but he'll live."

"Can he come home today?" Nik asked.

"Yes, actually. His arm is already set with a cast and his ribs taped. He's in a lot of pain, so I'm sending him home with some pain meds. Your poor mother was a wreck when she brought him in. She hasn't even recovered from her own injury. I finally convinced her to go home, and I said I would call her later with an update."

"Yeah, she just called me, so that's why I came in."

"You can save your mother a trip if you'd like to hang around for a bit." Doc looked at Nik in question.

Nik looked at me with raised eyebrows, and I nodded. "We can do that," he replied. "We'll just go down and get something to eat from the cafeteria."

"Sounds good. I'll get the documents finalized for his release and have you paged when he's ready to go home." He started to walk away.

"Thanks, Doc. I really appreciate it," Nik hollered after him.

"No problem. Give your mother my best."

"Will do."

Doc left and Nik and I headed downstairs.

"Jail might not be a bad place for Viggo." Nik's jaw bulged once before he added, "He needs a set of bars to save him from himself, apparently. I don't know what's going on with him, but he is definitely not acting normal."

"I know I didn't know him before now, but I got that impression as well. He just seems unsettled. I don't think he's the killer, yet he seems nervous."

"Agreed." Nik scrubbed a hand through his thick waves.

We had reached the lobby floor and were about to head down the hall to the cafeteria when an ambulance came barreling into the driveway. Sirens wailed and doctors went running. We stepped back out of the way as a stretcher whizzed by with a woman on it.

I did a double take.

"Is that...?" I asked with wide eyes.

"It sure is," Nik answered with a frown.

Scout Armstrong looked pale and unresponsive.

"Hey," Nik stepped in front of Max Rowland, who was an EMT and our friend. "What happened?"

"Carbon Monoxide poisoning." Max rubbed a hand over his sandy blond flattop. "She brought her grill into her trailer to keep warm. Unfortunately, she's not the first case we've had of it. Gonna be a long winter."

"Is she going to make it?" I asked.

His troubled gray eyes locked onto mine. "I don't know. What I do know is that something seemed off in her trailer. Winnie delivered her mail and had a package that needed to be signed for. She saw her door cracked open, but when she hollered for Scout, no one answered. She went inside and saw her passed out on the floor, so she called 911. She shut the grill off and waited outside until the paramedics arrived."

"Did anything look unusual to you?" Nik asked.

Max shook his head. "I'm no doctor, but she sure looked like she'd gotten knocked over the head to me. And not the kind of bump you get from a fall on your carpeted floor." He shrugged. "I gotta run. Give your families my best." He nodded to us both and headed down the hall.

"What on earth do you think that means?" I looked at Nik.

"That Scout's trailer just became a crime scene."

~

"I WOULD LIKE to buy a round of tequila shots for my girls," Jaz announced the next night at Flannigan's Pub.

The Irish bar had a singer in one corner playing the guitar and singing classic Irish tunes. Lots of stained wood, warm yellow lighting, and framed pictures of Ireland filled the pub, lending a homey atmosphere.

Eleni, Thalia, Winnie, and I all sat at the bar. Zena was manning the bar because she had to work. She took her break to join us in a celebratory shot.

"Okay, Jazlynn Alvarez, enough with the suspense. Exactly what are we celebrating?" I asked.

"Boomer asked me to marry him, and I said yes." She thrust out her ring finger which had a huge teardrop diamond with amber stones that matched her eyes on each side, encased in a platinum setting. The ring was as stunning as her, and my heart sang with happiness for my best friend.

We all cheered and squealed.

"Bottoms up, ladies." Zena held up her glass. "May you have a long, happy marriage, and big, healthy babies. Cheers to the bride to be."

We all licked the salt off the backs of our hand, tossed back our shots of tequila, and bit into our lemons. I only pretended to lick my hand, of course, cringing over the horrifying thought of how many germs were coursing over their tongues right now as I bit into my lemon and puckered my face.

Jaz raised a honey-colored, perfectly shaped brow at me.

I held up my empty glass and flashed her a lemony smile that said, *this one's for you.* I shuddered over the taste in my mouth. Give me wine any day of the week. I was not a shots kind of girl, and she knew it.

She rolled her eyes then gave me a wink.

"Details," Thalia said.

"Yeah, we want to live through you since we don't even have any men in our lives." Eleni chased her shot with a beer.

"Speak for yourself." Thalia's lips tipped up in a slight smile.

"Oooh, spill the tea, mate." Winnie rubbed her hands together.

"Senator Parker West, I take it," I said, not sure how I felt about that, and knowing Nik for certain wouldn't be happy.

"Maybe." Thalia played coy. "Nothing official yet, but things are heading in that direction. But enough about me. Let's get back to engagement details."

"Exactly." Zena slapped her shot glass on the bar. "I could use some tips on how to get *my* man headed in that direction before my break is over."

"Okay, okay." Jaz laughed in delight that made us all smile along with her. "Boomer was so incredibly sweet. I proposed to him so many times last year, but he's old-fashioned. He wanted to be the one to propose to me instead, but I didn't think he would ever get around to doing it. What can I say? I'm impatient. When I know I want something, I go after it full throttle."

"We know." I laughed.

"Ha-ha. Okay, so, I came home from work last night to candles, romantic music, champagne, and my favorite dinner—takeout, of course." She chuckled. "Boomer can't cook any better than I can. Anyway, Boomer is always doing sweet romantic things, so I didn't think anything of it. We were talking about our plans for the year, and he got up to serve us dessert, which I'd scarfed down before he'd even gotten back to the table with our cappuccinos."

"That's such a Jazism. Jaz doesn't mess around when it comes to food and she's hungry," I said. "Trust me, I know from experience. A hangry Jaz is scary."

"You're just full of laughs tonight." Jaz gave me a mock scowl. "Careful, darling, or I'll reveal some Kallisms."

"Touche." I held up my hands and laughed.

"Back to me." She grinned wide. "Boomer might not be able to cook, but one thing he *can* do is make amazing cappuccinos. He made us both our coffee with foam and swirled caramel just how I like it and set mine in front of me. I had almost taken a sip, when he stopped me and said, *aren't you going to look at the fancy swirl I gave you? I'm getting pretty good these days, if I do say so myself.* I laughed as I glanced down into my cup, then gasped." Jaz paused for dramatic effect, of course.

"What was in there? I'm on the edge of my seat." Thalia literally leaned so far forward she almost fell off her stool.

Jaz beamed as she finished with, "Swirled into the white foam was caramel lettering that said, *Marry me?*"

"Oh my gosh, how adorable." Eleni clapped her hands. "Why can't I have a man like that?"

"What did you do?" Winnie asked with wide eyes.

"I dropped my cup, screamed yes, and then knocked him over as I threw myself into his arms and kissed his whole face."

"That is such a Jaz thing to do. I love it." I giggled, finding myself wrapped up in the excitement of the moment as well. Jaz's recantation was the next best thing to being there with all the details and drama she added. Normally, I didn't like drama, but in this case, we were all enchanted.

"Hurry up, my break is almost over. I have to know. How did he give you the ring—which is gorgeous by the way?" Zena asked.

"Thank you. I love it. Anway, we were both sprawled out on the floor, so of course Chanel and Versace came running over to lick our faces. That's when I noticed the ring tied in red satin ribbon to Chanel's collar and a single red rose tied to Versace's collar. I absolutely adore that he included our babies in the proposal. My man knows me so well."

"That he does," I said. "I am genuinely so very happy for you both."

"I know. Me too." Jaz squealed and gave me a hug, holding on a moment longer than normal. *Um, look towards the corner of the bar. What in the world is he doing here and with her no less?*

I pulled back casually because the other girls had stopped talking and I could feel them staring at us oddly.

"Next rounds on me," I said.

They all cheered as Zena went back to work behind the bar, filling their orders.

Meanwhile, I turned to look in the corner of the bar like Jaz had suggested. My lips parted and jaw fell open. Viggo had just gotten out of the hospital yesterday with fractured ribs and a broken arm. What on earth was he doing in a bar while on pain meds? Even more confusing was why he was with her of all people.

Zelda Knight.

They sat at a cozy table for two. He had a beer before him. Not a very smart decision. She had a martini. I watched them talking. She was all smiles and animated, while he stared straight ahead, nodding once or twice, but definitely not smiling. He didn't look very happy to be with her.

I glanced around the room until my gaze landed on the person I was searching for.

Knox Young.

He sat at a table across the room, talking intensely to a man I didn't recognize. The man was tall with an athletic build. He was well-dressed with slicked back gray hair in a man bun. Definitely someone I would have recognized seeing before. Then again, a lot of tourists were in town for the Winter Carnival.

Clearview always held their annual Winter Carnival right after the new year before the winter solstice ended. There were snowmobile and cross-country ski races, sledding and sled dog races, speed and figure skating competitions, a chili cookoff, and of course, the snow angel and snowman competition. A parade concluded the festivities. It was quite a festival, but that wasn't what I was thinking about at the moment.

So many questions ran through my mind, the most puzzling being:

Why was Viggo with Zelda if he wasn't happy with her?

Who was this suave man?

How did this stranger know Knox?

I shot off a text to Nik. One thing was certain. Viggo was going to jail if we didn't get some answers soon.

I sat on the couch at Nik's place in my flannel pajamas, staring into a crackling fire he had started. My fuzzy sock clad feet were propped up on his coffee table with Wolfgang snoring softly beneath my legs. I now carried a lint roller along with my hand sanitizer.

Just the thought of going to bed with dog hairs between my sheets made my skin crawl.

Wolf and I understood each other. He knew better than to rub up against me, and I gave him extra pets on his huge head. It was a good thing my mind-reading ability didn't work on animals. I wasn't at all sure I wanted to know what he thought of my quirks.

Whenever I came over to stay, Wolf was my shadow. He felt the need to protect me, and I found that endearing. I didn't know if I would ever get used to his slobbering, but the massive Saint Bernard had stolen a place in my heart.

Nik walked over and handed me a glass of chardonnay then popped open a longneck as he sat next to me in the matching flannel pajamas I'd bought him. He wasn't a pajama sort of guy, but he wore them when he knew I was coming over.

I found that even more endearing.

I had to admit I had some pretty special guys in my life. If only Ms. Priss would warm up to them both, I could seriously consider knocking down that wall between us. First things first, Nik needed to trust me enough to knock down his own walls. It really bothered me that he didn't. How were we supposed to move forward without trust?

"Can I ask you something?" I leaned my head on his shoulder.

"Anything." He slipped his arm around me. *As long as you don't read my mind.*

"I'm not trying to, I promise." I moved away from him to prove my point.

He frowned. "I was half kidding. What's got you so serious?"

I chewed my lip for a minute, trying to find the right words. "Why won't you tell me what happened between you and Viggo in the past?"

Nik hesitated a moment and then pinched the top of his nose between his eyes. He took a big swig of his drink. "It's not that I'm purposely keeping something from you. I just don't like talking about that part of my life."

I waited patiently, listening.

"I was engaged before."

I blinked and my lips parted. "Y-You were?" I hadn't expected that. Why hadn't he told me, and how did I feel about that?

He nodded slowly.

"What happened?" I asked softly.

"It was a long time ago." He gave me a look that said, *I know what you're thinking.* "It has nothing to do with you, I just don't like to talk about it. That's the *only* reason I haven't. I was young and foolish and in love. Morgan was in the academy with me. I brought her home on break to meet the family."

"Wow, that's a big step," I said, realizing he hadn't brought me home to meet his family yet. At least not on his father's side.

"So, I thought." He rubbed the back of his neck.

"What happened?"

"Everything went great. My whole family loved her. We went back to start our new jobs on the force in Boston. I proposed, and she said yes. We were happy, living together, and planning our wedding."

"I don't understand. What went wrong?"

"Viggo showed up." Nik's jaw hardened.

"He's your cousin." I curled my feet beneath me and looked up at him. "Why should that make a difference?"

"Exactly. It *shouldn't* make a difference." Nik stared into the fire, watching the flames flicker. "Viggo had an acting gig. A small role in a movie. I was deep undercover on a case, so I couldn't see or talk to Morgan much. When the case was solved, I came home to find she had moved out, leaving me a note that said she called off the wedding."

I sucked in a sharp breath. "Oh, no. Why?"

"Said she never really loved me." Nik cracked his neck. "Apparently, she realized that because of the way she felt for Viggo."

My heart ached for him. "I'm so sorry, Nik. That's terrible. What did Viggo have to say about it?"

Nik finished his beer with one long swallow and set the longneck on the end table. "He claims she came onto him. That he turned her down, but she told him we had ended things right before I went on the job. She moved out to prove it to him, so he figured there was no harm in him taking her up on her offer."

"Even if all that were true, there was definite harm." I couldn't imagine being betrayed by my own family. "You're his cousin. His flesh and blood. His *family*. What he did was wrong on so many levels."

"I said the same thing back then." Nik laughed harshly. then a sad look crossed over his face. "Viggo didn't understand it then and still doesn't understand now why I will never think of him the same way again."

"I don't blame you." I brushed a lock of his hair off his forehead, and he snagged my wrist, and kissed my hand.

*I'm so lucky to have you.*

"I'm the lucky one." I cupped his cheek then pulled a blanket over my lap. "Whatever happened between Viggo and Morgan?"

"He was only looking for a good time. He dumped her like I knew he would as soon as his movie was finished filming. She tried to come back to me. Her version of the story was that he seduced her, knowing we were still together. We hadn't broken up, but she said Viggo didn't care. Of course, he denies it, but it really doesn't matter whose story is the right one. Neither one of them deserved to be in my life after that. Solving this case is my job, but I'm not trying to clear Viggo's name for him. I'm doing it for my aunt and uncle."

Wolfgang whined, stood up, and licked Nik's hand.

Nik smiled fondly and rubbed the dog's head. "I'm okay, buddy."

Now I understood why Nik was wary if I so much as looked at Viggo. He just had no idea that no man would ever compare to him. "I love you," I said softly.

His piercing blue eyes met mine and softened. "I

love you, too." He leaned forward and kissed me softly. *So damn much.*

I smiled against his lips before leaning back. "So, guess what happened tonight at the bar?"

"What?" He eyed me curiously.

"Jaz got engaged."

His grin widened. "So, Boomer finally popped the question? He told me he was going to. Did he do the coffee swirl thing?"

"Yes, how did you know?"

"He's been practicing a lot and drinking the evidence." Nik chuckled. "Talk about being wired. I don't think I could take much more."

"Her ring is beautiful. I'm so happy for them."

"Same." Nik just stared at me.

"I don't need to touch you to read your mind, you know."

"And...?"

"And we need to solve this case before considering moving in together or anything else, for that matter."

His eyes narrowed. "We?"

I ignored his comment by asking a question of my own. "Guess what else happened at the bar tonight?"

He let it go on a sigh. "Enlighten me."

"Viggo was there."

Nik's full lips parted then flattened into a hard line. "What was he doing in a bar in his condition?"

"Drinking a beer with Zelda at a cozy little table."

"The man's carelessness astounds me." Nik's anger turned to confusion. "I thought Zelda was with Knox?"

"I don't know what Zelda and Knox are, but they are most definitely not a couple. Knox was also there but he was with this older, suave, well-dressed man I've never seen before. He had gray-streaked hair and a man bun. Then again, the Winter Carnival has started, so we do have a lot more strangers in town."

"Which makes solving this case even harder. Captain Crenshaw has been riding Boomer and I hard to wrap this up." Nik's face looked pensive. "You're not the only one who had an eventful evening tonight."

"Really, do tell." I wagged my eyebrows.

"Scout Armstrong woke up."

I sat up straight. "Seriously? We should go see her."

"*We* aren't going anywhere." He tweaked my nose with his index finger. "But I did already go talk to her."

I swatted his hand away, ignoring his emphasis on we. "Did you tell her what Winnie found and what Max said?"

"I *am* a detective, Ballas," Nik said dryly. "Do you want to hear the rest of my story, or what?"

"I know, I know. Sorry. I just get excited. Go ahead." I made a motion like my lips were zipped.

"Scout is a pretty tough woman. She can take care of herself. And she's no fool. She never would have brought her grill inside to heat her trailer. But she was desperate. She admitted that she followed Delilah home."

"But Delilah didn't go home."

"Scout didn't know that. She thought Dixie's house was Delilah's, so when Scout saw the lights on in the upstairs, she knew Viggo would keep Delilah busy for hours. So, she snuck in to look around."

"Do you think she killed her?"

"She claims she didn't. She said she wanted to find something of value that she could pawn since she figured Delilah owed her the rest of the money they agreed on for her services at the New Year's Eve party."

"That explains the drawers being a mess and

things overturned, but Dixie claims nothing was missing."

"Because Scout was interrupted. She said she was snooping around when she heard a noise coming from the back door. The same door she'd let herself in through. There was no break in because she'd seen Delilah fish the key out of a fake rock key holder. So, she used that and left the door unlocked while she snooped."

"If the noise came from the back door, it couldn't have been Delilah coming down the stairs."

"Exactly. Someone else came in the already unlocked door."

"Oh goodness, what did Scout do?"

"Said she stayed in the shadows until the person was in the other room. Then she quickly slipped back out the door and went home."

"Did she see what they looked like?"

"No, she only saw a shadow. But that doesn't mean the killer didn't see her. That would explain them going to her trailer, knocking her out, then ransacking her place."

"Maybe the killer really was looking for something and not just after Delilah."

"Maybe." He scooped me into his arms and headed toward his bedroom.

"What are you doing?" I laughed.

He kissed me. *Taking your mind off going places it shouldn't.*

"W-What were we talking about?" I muttered against his lips.

He chuckled. *Success.* Then he kicked the door closed behind us, and I forgot my own name.

❧

IT WAS A BRIGHT, sunny day and Clearview Park, located at the end of Main Street on the edge of town, was packed with people attending the Winter Carnival. Nik and Boomer dropped Wolfgang, Chanel, and Versace off at the fenced-in dog park on the edge of the park.

Milly Donovan volunteered to dog-sit so others could enjoy the festival. Her new husband, Nelson Rockwell, of Rockwell Jewelers stood by her side. Milly was a petite redhead with pale green eyes. She'd stolen the heart of the uptight jewelry store owner with his light brown lacquered hair and side part. He'd recently surprised her with a fabulous engagement ring, and they were married quickly in a small ceremony because neither one had wanted to wait.

Romance was definitely in the air in Clearview this new year.

Jaz and I passed by the playground full of screaming and giggling children, and we stopped by the food trucks to get some hot chocolate. Finally, we reached the pavilion where most events were held, and, soon after, our men joined us.

"Hi, Kalli, I was hoping you would be here," Sherry Harper said. "Bennett extended our trip. Isn't that wonderful?"

"That's great news." I watched Bennett and another sophisticated couple walking towards us. "I'm so glad you're enjoying our town. Who are your friends?"

She peeked over her shoulder and beamed. "Bennett ran into some fellow philanthropists he knows from the city. They heard about the Winter Carnival and came to check it out just as we were leaving. I had already asked Bennett to stay, but he wanted to get home to work on one of his many projects. They helped me seal the deal by convincing him to stay. They're really nice people."

"Kalli, Jaz, Nik, and Boomer, I would like you to meet Yvonne and Humphry Rigsby." Shelly gestured to the dashing couple who looked to be a little younger than Bennett and her but equally sophisticated.

"It's a pleasure to meet you." Humphry's chestnut brown curls were perfectly trimmed as he nodded to the men, shaking their hands, and smiled at me and Jaz with friendly dark brown eyes.

Thank goodness he didn't try to shake my hand. I kept my gloves on just in case.

"Charmed, ladies." Yvonne's sleek black bob was tucked behind her ears. Her pale gray eyes swiveled over to Nik and Boomer. "Gentlemen." She tilted her head ever so slightly, her deep red lips tipping up at the corners.

"Good to meet you all," Boomer said.

Nik's cell phone buzzed. He read the text. "It's Captain," he said to Boomer. "Disturbing the peace over by the races." He looked at the others. "Duty calls."

"They're detectives," I said as Boomer and Nik left to catch up with Captain Crenshaw by the snowmobile races. "They're a little short staffed at the moment because of the murder, unfortunately." The moment I said the word murder, I realized my mistake.

Yvonne and Humphry looked at each other.

"Very nice to meet you both." Jaz changed the subject. We couldn't afford for people to get scared off when the town relied on the profit from the carnival. "If you are in the mood to shop while you're here, pop on over to Full Disclosure. I'm sure I can hook you up with something fabulous."

"I'll keep that in mind," Yvonne said.

"And Kalli here has some incredible lingerie she designs," Jaz added. "Award winning, in fact."

I blushed. Good Lord, I hated promoting my designs because I didn't like drawing attention to myself.

"I'll definitely keep *that* in mind." Humphry elbowed Bennett.

Bennett cleared his throat. "Yes, well, we should probably head over across the way and check out the craft tents. The people here are so very talented. You never know what gem you might find."

"Oh, I do love a good gem." Sherry looped her arm through Yvonne's as they walked away. "You should see the antique jewelry box Bennett got me for our anniversary. The craftsmanship is remarkable, and it has this adorable little trap door."

"Well, what do you want to do now?" Jaz asked.

"Let's go see what disturbed the peace," I answered.

We headed over to where the snowmobile and cross-country ski races were supposed to be taking place. Halfway there, we stopped in our tracks.

There were dogs running loose everywhere.

"Oh, no!" Jaz stared with her mouth agape.

Boomer chased Chanel and Versace, who leapt like graceful gazelles, terrified of all the disorderly conduct. Nik bolted after Wolfgang, who was being a naughty boy and loving every minute of it. He stole food, played with crafts like they were toys, and tugged at tents in a game of war. It was worse than a herd of buffalo.

Tents got knocked over.

People got trampled.

Chaos ensued.

I looked around for the guilty culprit. Aunt Tasoula ran around screaming her head off as if the dogs were rabid instead of the friendly neighborhood pets.

"Cujo! It's Cujo! Save me, Ares! I make it worth your while." She jumped onto Tate's back.

Ares was the Greek god of war. Tate looked like a god, but he was merely her massive mortal boyfriend.

"Oh, woe is me. He has the foam of the mouth disease. The raspberries." She pointed at Wolfgang. "He going to eat me! I too pretty to die."

"I got you, love." Tate ran around like a centaur with, Aunt Tasoula clinging to his long hair like reins, screaming for him to go faster.

The man was a saint.

Wolfgang always drooled. He wasn't foaming at the mouth, for Zeus's sake, but there was no convincing her he wasn't rabid. YiaYia Dido chased Frona as she lassoed and rode a Great Dane for eight seconds, then leapt off and bowed to the crowd. Captain Crenshaw held Chloe in his arms, her crutches in the mouths of twin Bull Mastiffs who were making snow art as they ran in circles dragging them behind.

Senator Parker West shook his head, taking notes and making phone calls. Mayor Flynn Zimmerman was yelling orders to Nik, Boomer, and the captain. Pop, Papou, Jasper, my cousins, and both Fathers all did their part in trying to fix what was ruined.

But there was one person who stood off to the side, doing nothing but inspecting her nails.

I marched over to her. "Ma! What did you do?" I crossed my arms over my chest and tapped my foot.

"Why you point that finger at me?" She tried for indignation. "You not nice to you poor mama."

I wasn't buying it. "You have guilt written all over your face, Ma. There's nothing poor about you."

"I no have guilt on my face." She paused a beat, then threw up her hands. "It's no my fault."

"Aha, I knew it! Any time there's trouble, either you or Aunt Tasoula are involved." I rubbed my throbbing temples before asking, "If all this chaos is not your fault, Ma, then who's fault is it?"

"Planetarium," she said emphatically. "That nasty goblin deceived you all. He transform into animals, you know. I tell by the way that dog look at me."

"What dog?" My head was pounding now.

She pointed to a little chihuahua, wearing a sweater and booties. He curled up in a pile of hay waiting for his owner to come fetch him. If I wasn't mistaken, his owner was the little old lady town librarian.

"Seriously? What harm can that tiny little dog possibly do, Ma?"

"He growl at me. I know that growl. He a goblin. I fix him. I open the gate to shoo him away. I no help it the other dogs push their way out. I could have been hurt. They all untrained, crazy beasts. Stick with cats."

"They're not crazy, Ma. *You* are. And I'm pretty sure you're going to be in big trouble now."

"Bah." She waved her hand through the air. "You Pop fix it."

"You just might have done something even Pop can't fix this time."

For the first time in this conversation...Ma looked worried.

## 10

The next morning, I carried a bag of money from my lingerie sales at Full Disclosure into Clearview National Bank to be deposited into my account. The bank was busy this morning. While I was standing in line waiting for my turn at the teller, I thought about Ma.

Pop was not happy with her. He had to use money from the restaurant to pay for damages to the Winter Carnival tents and supplies. She was lucky no pet owner had pressed charges against her.

Of course, she blamed the mess on the goblins.

Sighing, I checked my watch. I'd been waiting for ten minutes. Glancing around, I turned my head back to an office with a glass wall. My eyes widened. Andrew Ledger was president of the bank. He didn't handle the day-to-day operations, so what was Cameron Oswald doing in his office?

The bell over the front door chimed and drew my attention. Dixie Doolittle marched inside, and she didn't look happy. When she spotted Andrew, she stormed over to his office and whipped open the door without a single knock.

"You have no right," she shouted.

"What are you talking about? I have every right. I was Delilah's assistant. It's only natural I take over her business." Cameron sat up straighter.

"I'm not talking to you," Dixie clarified. "I could care less about her little party planning business."

"Then who are you talking to?" Cameron asked.

"Him." Dixie stabbed a finger in Andrew's direction.

"Cameron, we'll finish our negotiation another time if you don't mind." Andrew closed a folder he had before him.

"Certainly." She gathered her things and gave Dixie a wide berth as she stepped around her and quickly exited the bank.

"Please, sit down, and we'll discuss this like adults." He gestured toward the chair across from his desk that Cameron had just vacated.

"Don't tell me what to do," Dixie said through her teeth. "My sister had me as her beneficiary until she met you."

"We were engaged. Of course she would change her beneficiary to me. You were the one who caused the rift between you two. Not me." He started putting files on his desk away. "If that's all."

"Hardly! I warned her to stay away from you. That you were no good, but she wouldn't listen. And then you cheated on her with Bessie Halifax of all people. You knew that would kill Delilah."

His face flushed red, and he surged to his feet. "Bessie seduced me, not the other way around."

"You didn't have to give in."

"I'm just a man." His shoulders slumped, and he sat back down. "I'm human and made a mistake. Delilah was going to give me a second chance until that Viking came to town." Andrew's face hardened.

"And now the love of my life is dead. He's the one you should be angry at, not me."

"Delilah and I made up. She was never going to get back with you, and she told me she was going to put me back as her beneficiary. She took out a big life insurance policy when you two got engaged. And now, suddenly, she's dead. I think you talked her into adding the policy and then you killed her when you realized she wasn't going to take you back before she had a chance to change her policy back to me." Dixie slapped a hand on his desk. "That money's mine, not yours. You have no right to it."

"You're crazy, and I want you out of my office now, or I'm going to call the police." He picked up his phone.

"Gladly. This isn't over." She pointed her finger in his face again. "You'll be hearing from my lawyer soon." Dixie stormed back out of the bank as quickly as she had stormed in, leaving a path of destruction like a hurricane along the way.

"Next," the teller said, snapping my attention back in front of me.

I deposited my money and turned around to leave the bank when in walked Bessie Halifax herself. She entered Andrew's office and closed the door like it was the most natural thing in the world for her to do.

This day just kept getting more and more interesting.

~

"Hey, the sun's out. Do you want to go for a walk?" I asked Jaz while we were at work. She had help to run the shop, so we could take breaks whenever we wanted to.

"Sure," she said. "I could use a break; just let me get my coat."

Five minutes later, after grabbing an afternoon coffee and tea across the street, from Maria at Simply Delicious, we headed down the street. It felt good to be outside and clear my head. We passed by all sorts of shops and little cafes through the business district in silence, sipping our drinks and soaking up the sun.

Jaz and I had that kind of friendship. There was never an awkward silence. We simply were so comfortable with each other that sometimes no words were necessary. The streets were full of tourists and the Winter Carnival activities were still going on.

"So how are wedding plans going?" I finally asked.

"Ugh, I have so many ideas, but of course, Boomer is no help in narrowing them down. All he says is, *whatever you want, babe.*"

"That's not uncommon. A lot of men aren't into planning that sort of thing. Be happy he's not disagreeing with you on what you want."

"Oh, I'm sure that time is coming. I have a lot of ideas, and some of them are expensive. I'm sure then I'll get the argument, *is this really necessary*? He's so practical. I only plan on getting married once, so I want what I want."

"Knowing you, I'm sure you'll get it."

"What kind of wedding would you want?"

My heart flipped over the thought of walking down an aisle with all eyes on me. "A simple one." Or none at all.

"Good luck with that, given your family."

"No kidding. They'll be arguing with me that I'm not spending enough. You know how they are. They go over the top for everything. You should see what they are planning for Jasper's adoption."

Jaz arched an eyebrow all the way to her hairline and choked on her coffee. "Isn't he like twenty-seven?"

"Yes. Exactly. Way too old to be adopted." I shook my head on a laugh. "They are insane, but you gotta love them."

"What does Jasper think of it?" Jaz resumed sipping her coffee, albeit a bit more carefully.

I thought about that for a moment. "Honestly, he doesn't seem to mind the attention one bit."

"Probably because he went his whole life without it."

"That's true. I'm happy for him." I sipped my tea. "I'm just glad the attention isn't on me. Thank the Lord I don't have to worry about an engagement any time soon."

"What about moving in together? Any progress there?"

"We agreed to talk about it after this case is solved. Right now, neither one of us can focus on anything except clearing Viggo's name."

"Speaking of Viggo," Jaz held up her hand to shield her eyes from the sun, "isn't that him up ahead?"

I looked to where she pointed and shielded my own eyes to see better. And what I saw was not good. "That's sure not Zelda that he's with."

Jaz gasped. "Oh boy. That's Theresa Finley." She looked at me with eyes sprung wide. "Does the man have a death wish?"

"I think he just might."

Viggo and Theresa were standing outside of Finley's Finds. Theresa's husband Mack was a lumberjack, and she owned this pawn shop. We hurried our steps to catch up to them before Viggo did something stupid.

Too late.

Viggo and Theresa had their heads bent together, looking at something, having no idea of the tornado headed their way. Mack Finley was stomping his way down the street from the opposite direction.

"Hurry," I said to Jaz.

"Easier said than done in these boots."

"Don't you own anything that doesn't have high heels?"

"Hey, wear it while you can. That's my motto."

We reached Viggo's side a few seconds before Mack.

"Viggo, look out," I yelled then quickly dialed Nik and filled him in.

Viggo turned with surprised eyes and ducked just as Mack swung. Viggo was six-foot-five and Mack looked to be the same height. Viggo was all sculpted muscle, but Mack had a thick powerful body and no broken arm or cracked ribs.

"Hey, man, what's wrong with you?" Viggo stumbled back a couple steps away, breathing hard.

"You bloody well won't stay away from my wife," Mack spat. "That's what's wrong with me."

"He didn't do anything wrong." Theresa covered her head and cowered when Mack spun around on her.

"I ain't talking to you, woman."

Jaz stepped in front of Theresa and raised her chin a notch. "Well, I'm talking to *you*, buddy, and I suggest you back off. My fiancé's a detective, and he doesn't take kindly to men who bully their women."

"You don't know what you're talking about."

"The bruises on her arms say otherwise." I joined Jaz in front of Theresa. "And my boyfriend is a detective and cousin to the man you are attempting to harm."

"*He's* the one who harms people." Mack thrust his finger in Viggo's direction. "Poor Delilah is dead, and he seduced my wife. Now he's coming back for more. He wants more? I'll give him more."

"I didn't seduce anyone." Viggo threw up his one good arm. "She told me she was single."

Mack whipped his head around to glare at Theresa.

Theresa whimpered.

"Sorry, Theresa," Viggo said to her and winced.

Sirens wailed and Nik and Boomer pulled up at the same time.

"Everything okay?" Boomer asked Jaz as he rolled his body out of his car and strode over to her in record time.

"Everything's just fine, honey." Jaz put her hands on her hips. "We've got things under control here. Don't we, Kalli?"

"We sure do." I crossed my arms and glared at Mack.

"That's what I'm afraid of." Nik joined us and faced his cousin. "Viggo, what did you do this time?"

"I swear I didn't do anything wrong."

"I've heard that before. Why are you here?"

"He was just checking to see how much his pocket watch would be worth," Theresa said, peeking out at her husband. "I swear that was all. We were only doing business. I do own a pawn shop, Mack."

"I'll deal with you later," Mack said, keeping his eyes locked on Viggo.

"Is what she said true?" Nik asked Viggo with his hands on his hips and eyebrows rising up to his hairline.

Viggo couldn't quite meet Nik's eyes. He nodded once without saying a word.

"Why would you sell your bestefar's watch? That's all you have left of him." Nik dropped his hands, looking shocked and confused.

"Bestefar?" Jaz whispered to me. "Who's that?"

"His grandfather."

"I wasn't going to really sell it." Viggo brushed off his concern. "I was just interested in finding out how much it was worth. You know, for insurance purposes."

"Right," Nik ground out, looking back to Mack. "I trust there won't be another incident with you, Mr. Finley. Am I correct?"

Mack's jaw bulged. "Fine, I'll leave the coward alone. But he best stay far away from me and what's mine."

"Oh, I'll make sure of that." Nik shot a meaningful look at Viggo before looking back at Mack. "You have my word."

"And you have *my* word that if I get another domestic violence complaint about you from anyone, I have a cell with your name on it, ready and waiting. Did I mention my uncle owns the logging company you work for?" Boomer shrugged nonchalantly, but the look in his eyes was cold and hard. "Small world, isn't it?"

No more words were necessary.

Mack stormed off in the direction he came from.

"Thank you all." Theresa folded her arms over her middle in a gesture that looked like she did that often.

"You don't have to take his abuse, you know," Jaz said.

"There are people who can help," I added.

"Oh, Mack's more bark than bite." Theresa laughed lightly, but she didn't look us in the eye.

"If you ever need anything, call me." Boomer handed her his card.

"Or me." Nik handed her his card as well.

She nodded and took the cards.

Nik turned to Viggo. "I'll give you a ride home."

"That's okay, I can walk."

"Actually, it's not okay, and we need to talk." Nik opened the door to his car, and Viggo only hesitated a moment before climbing inside.

"As for you, I thought I asked you not to interfere in this case?" Nik stared at me with weariness, looking tired.

"I promise you; I wasn't looking for trouble." My voice rang with sincerity. "Jaz and I went for a walk, that's all."

Jaz nodded. "She's telling the truth."

"Then I guess it doesn't matter what you're doing, because apparently trouble seems to find you wherever you are. And that's enough."

## 11

That evening, the chili cookoff was in full swing at the Winter Carnival, and the temperature had dropped, making the demand for the hot dish increase sales considerably. My parents could barely keep up.

It was my turn to take a shift in volunteering to run Aphrodite's booth on Restaurant Row. I hadn't seen Nik since he'd taken Viggo home in the afternoon. I had to admit I was curious what they talked about.

Had Viggo really been trying to pawn his grandfather's watch? If so, why?

Viggo had to make a decent enough living with all the modeling shoots and commercials he did. So why would he want to part with the last thing his grandfather gave him before he died? It was his grandfather on his mother's side, so it wasn't Nik's grandfather, but I could tell the thought bothered Nik a lot.

He was a sentimental sort, and I loved that about him.

"Frona, you naughty girl. Get back here with that ladle." YiaYia chased my cousin out from under our tent.

Frona held her trophy high, singing, "Malaganas took my rosy jelly, I whack him in his big, fat belly."

"Those goblins ruin everything," Ma said. "If I lose this cookoff to Vincenzo Ricci, it will be the goblin's fault."

Ma and Vinnie had come to a truce of sorts, but he would always be her competition with his Italian restaurant and their traditional chili. Flannigan's Pub also had a booth with his secret recipe chili. Diner Delights had a booth with Mediterranean style chili. And Rosalita's had a booth with her Texas Chili. Maria had a Sinfully Delicious booth, offering desserts and coffee samples, but she wasn't part of the chili cookoff.

The judges hadn't come by yet, and Ma had been cooking all day. Jaz was manning our Full Disclosure and Kalli Originals booth on Looter's Lane this evening while I was helping my parents out. The Winter Carnival was packed.

Anastasia Stewart, who owned a clothing boutique called Vixen's, had a booth on Looter's Lane as well. She was our direct competition and formerly Jaz's arch nemesis, but they had called a truce of their own. *Friendly* competition kept them both sharp.

Dixie had a Dixie's Doodad's booth with her antiques. Aunt Tasoula had a Hera's Halo booth with her salon products. Even Theresa had a Finley's Finds booth, offering services to pawn items or purchase item's she'd acquired.

Her husband Mack was nowhere in sight, thank goodness.

My phone buzzed.

I glanced at it. Nik had texted me that he and Boomer were here and would meet me at the food tents for dinner. Meanwhile, Lois Flannigan came walking over with

Sherry and Yvonne with a big smile on her face. She loved gossip and being a part of what she considered the "in" crowd whenever someone new came to town.

Lois and her husband, Michael, were never blessed with children. He worked long hours at his pub, and he wanted her to be happy. So, she was the queen of Clearview's society, up on the latest news. And if there was a sale happening, she knew about it first.

Her rosy cheeks glowed and her eyes sparkled as she tucked her red hair beneath her winter cap and rubbed her hands together. "Brrrr, it's getting cold out."

"It sure is. Nice to see you ladies." I smiled in return.

"I'd like you to meet my new friends, Sherry and Yvonne." Lois beamed, gesturing to the women beside her.

"I've already had the honor." I nodded to both women.

"Yes, Kalli has been so good to me since I arrived in town." Sherry winked at me. "I really appreciate the warm welcome and helpful tips."

"It's been my pleasure."

"I'm rather new to town, but I have to say, the experience has been interesting to say the least." Yvonne eyed Ma warily.

"Oh, my word, I know," Lois said. "Wasn't that just crazy? Those poor snowmen didn't stand a chance. If they weren't getting decapitated, they were getting treated like fire hydrants, if you know what I mean." Lois cackled. "It certainly gave new meaning to that song, *Who Let the Dogs Out*."

"Indeed," Yvonne agreed, but obviously didn't find

it nearly as amusing, judging by the sour expression on her face.

"Can I interest you in some of our delicious chili?" I pulled on fresh plastic gloves, hoping to divert the conversation before Ma overheard them. "My parents outdid themselves this year." The smells wafting through the air had my stomach rumbling.

"Maybe just a taste," Lois said, lowering her voice, "but don't tell my Michael." She peeked down Restaurant Row, but Flannigan's Pub had a long line of their own.

I dished up three steaming bowls and put them each on a plate with a slice of thick, crusty, warm traditional Greek bread and a small cup of softened butter. "Here you go, ladies." I handed them the plates. "Enjoy."

"Thank you, Kalli. This looks wonderful." Sherry rubbed her hands together and eagerly took the plate from my hands.

"Yes, thank you. I'm starved." Yvonne took the plate and ate a spoonful right away, her eyes rolling back in heaven. "This is delicious."

"Thank you. Ma will be pleased to hear that. She's worked very hard on this year's entry in the competition." I wiped the counter in front of me with a disinfectant cloth. "So where are your husbands?"

"Working away." Lois sighed on a shrug and gestured towards her husband's booth. "That man works too hard. He's lucky I love him so darn much."

"Bennett and Humphry went to check out Dixie's antiques. Yvonne here loved my jewelry box, so I think Humphry wants to surprise her with something special, too." Sherry let out a dream sigh. "Isn't love grand?"

"Yes, well, they weren't very secretive about it, so it

won't exactly be a surprise," Yvonne said, adding, "but it's the thought that counts." She looked around, her eyes filling with the most interest I'd seen since I'd met her. "Where is the shopping section? I'd like to check out a few things myself."

"I'll leave you to Lois," I said as I spotted Nik headed my way. "You couldn't be in better hands."

Lois blushed and stood a little straighter as she nodded once at me, and then turned to the other women. "Come with me, ladies. I'll fix you right up. I have coupons." They threw their plates away and followed Lois.

"Hey, Ballas, what's cookin'?" Nikos the Greek came to a swaggering stop in front of the counter I stood behind, his full lips tipping up into a half-smile. He leaned his tall frame on the counter and winked at me.

He looked so handsome with his thick, wavy, coffee-colored hair slightly mussed, his olive skin still tan despite the winter. His chiseled face was heavily whiskered, revealing straight white teeth when he smiled wide.

Detective Stevens was all business, while Nik was the nice guy, but Nikos the Greek was pure naughtiness. His eyes were such a piercing blue and sparkled with mischief. They still made my heart flip every single time he looked at me.

And he knew it.

"I'd recommend the chili, *Detective*." I poured a bowl, added the bread and butter, and then handed him the plate.

I tried to act nonchalant like he didn't fluster me every time we were around each other. I'd known him for almost a year now, had been dating him for a few months, and we practically lived together. Yet the man could still turn my world upside down with a single smile.

Why did I let him drive me crazy?

He took the plate from me, and then leaned forward and kissed me. *For the record, you drive me crazy, too.* He leaned back and winked at me, then dug into his dinner.

I rolled my eyes.

"So, where's Boomer?"

"With Jaz at her Full Disclosure booth," he said between mouthfuls. "By the way, your valentine designs are sold out. I wonder who the special someone was for the inspiration for those?"

I blushed and could have kicked myself. "Gee, I wonder."

"He's a lucky guy."

"Where's Viggo?" I changed the subject.

Nikos laughed, then his smile slowly dimmed back to Nik. He tossed his plate in the trash before answering. "At Ma's house. She and the captain are here, but Viggo said he was tired. He wanted to rest. I made him promise not to drink this time while taking those pain meds. That can impair your judgment, but who knows if he'll listen."

"From what I've seen, he usually doesn't."

"Well, he'd better start because he's in enough trouble already."

The next morning, Nik's cell phone rang and woke us both up. I got up to feed Prissy while he answered his phone. I put the coffee on and made myself a cup of tea when he finally came walking out of my bedroom, fully dressed, with his badge and gun on.

"What's wrong?" I handed him the cup.

He took a big sip, looking at me over the rim of the cup with concern in his eyes. "Mack Finley is dead."

"What?" I gaped at him. "What happened?"

"Don't know." He lifted a shoulder and drank more coffee. "His wife says he never came home last night."

My forehead puckered. "Who found him?"

"Leonard Murphy showed up early this morning to do some maintenance work for Theresa at Finley's Finds, and he found Mack out back in the dumpster."

"That's crazy. We literally just saw him, and now he's dead in his wife's dumpster." I tried to wrap my brain around what was happening in Clearview. Two murders in such a short time. Were they related? "What did he die from?"

"Clint Davis the medical examiner says a knife wound."

I sucked in a sharp breath. "Do you think it's the same killer, or do we have two maniacs on the loose?"

"I'm not sure. The knife part is the same, but this time there was no murder weapon found. Maybe it's a copycat killer. Boomer's already there. I'm going to go talk to Theresa. Can you feed Wolf?"

I nodded. "Of course."

Nik finished his coffee then handed me his cup and kissed my cheek before heading out the door.

I quickly changed and fed Wolfgang, then locked up and headed out on a mission of my own.

A short time later, I pulled into Chloe's driveway. Most of the neighbors were away at work. Chloe's car was in the driveway, so I assumed she was home. I jogged up the steps and knocked on the door.

Viggo answered.

I waved.

He looked beyond me and then raised his brows

when he didn't see Nik. Stepping back, he opened the door wider as a slow grin spread across his face. "Come on in, then."

Maybe this wasn't such a good idea, I briefly thought before stepping inside.

He placed his hands on my shoulders. "Allow me." He started taking off my coat. *Can't get enough of me, love?*

"I've got it, thank you." I stepped away and slipped out of my coat, walking far around him and hanging it on a coat tree by the door. I slipped out of my boots and strode on sock feet into the kitchen. "Can you tell Aunt Chloe I'm here?"

"I would if I could, but she's not here."

I glanced toward the stairs to her bedroom. "But it's so early."

He lifted his hands, palms up. "She never came home last night."

"Oh...I thought because her car was here then she was as well." I looked around, not exactly sure if I should stay or go.

"I think she regrets letting me stay." Viggo's voice lost its flirtatiousness and rang with sincerity as he pulled his long, thick blond strands of hair into a man bun. "They don't really have any time alone with me here. I feel bad about that."

Maybe he wasn't such a bad guy, after all. Chloe obviously saw something good in him. "You could always move back in with Nik."

"Then *you* two wouldn't have any time alone." He started out sounding sincere, but then his striking blue eyes slid up to lock with mine. "Or is that what you want?"

So much for giving him the benefit of the doubt. "Listen, Viggo, I know what happened between you and Nik. Not a very nice thing to do to your cousin. Trust me, that's not going to happen this time."

His face hardened. "Morgan said they had broken things off before he left. It's not my fault she lied."

"That still doesn't make sleeping with your cousin's ex-fiancée right. What about bro code, not to mention, family loyalty."

A muscle in his jaw pulsed.

Tension filled the air between us, so I took a deep breath and reminded myself why I was there in the first place. I couldn't change the past, but he would never open up to me if I didn't change my tactic soon. For Chloe's sake and Viggo's parents, I needed to do my part in helping to clear their only son's name.

"Look, whatever differences you and Nik had in the past, you're still family. He's doing his best to keep you out of jail, but he needs your help."

Cockiness and anger left Viggo's face as his shoulders slumped. He leaned against the kitchen counter, folding his arms and crossing his ankles, as he stared off, concentrating. "I didn't kill Delilah. I don't remember much of what happened that night, but I do know I'm not a killer."

"I believe you." My gut told me he wasn't lying about that, at least. "Did you go anywhere last night?"

He narrowed his eyes and glanced into the living room. "I don't think so. I had a lot to drink, so last night is kind of a blur."

I looked at the empty beer bottles on the coffee table and raised a brow at him. "Aren't you on pain pills still?" And why was he drinking alone?

His eyes didn't meet mine. "I don't always take them."

"Well, that's good. That can be a dangerous mix." I wasn't sure I believed him. He was a big man. That still didn't seem like enough alcohol to make him forget what happened unless he mixed something with them and was lying about it.

"Why all the questions about last night?"

"Mack Finley was found dead in his wife's dumpster this morning."

Viggo's face paled. He started pacing back and forth. "That wasn't me. I swear it. I don't think I went anywhere. This is going to kill my mar."

I placed my hand on Viggo's arm. "Hey, it's okay. There's no use getting yourself all upset over what might not have happened."

His eyes met mine. *I can't go to jail, but Nikos will never help me if he knows the truth.* "I—I..."

"What's wrong?" I asked. "You can tell me."

"Just what the hell is going on here?" Nik asked from the doorway.

Viggo and I jerked apart.

"Nothing," Viggo said.

"Yeah, nothing," I repeated. Why was I blushing? I had nothing to feel guilty about...except interfering in his murder investigation again when I said I wouldn't.

"Funny, I've heard that one before." A look that I had never seen before and never wanted to see again entered Nik's eyes.

I suddenly felt like nothing was turning into something.

## 12

"I can't believe Nik is mad at me," I said to Jaz later that day. "Like really mad and distrustful. He can't possibly know me if he thinks I would ever betray him with anyone, let alone his cousin." I was pacing Jaz's apartment, growing angrier by the second.

"You told me about his past with his cousin," Jaz said gently.

I didn't tell anyone else, but she was my best friend and we shared everything. "Yeah, but that doesn't excuse his behavior."

"I'm just saying he might be overly sensitive where his cousin is concerned. Maybe he deserves a pass."

"I get that as an initial gut reaction and was more than willing to give him a pass. He pulled me aside, and we talked about it. I really thought that maybe he was just upset that I was sticking my nose in this investigation and trying to help him. Which I admitted I was. He knows about my mind-reading ability, so I told him I was only touching Viggo to get at the truth. He should have given *me* a pass for that."

"Very true." Jaz nodded.

"I was so close to getting Viggo to tell the truth before Nik came barging in." I placed my hands on my hips, still angry with my boyfriend. "Nik wouldn't listen to me. He didn't even let me tell him that Viggo was afraid Nik wouldn't help him if he knew the truth. Nik was so angry and irrational, he just stormed out and never let me finish. I don't even know if he's still my boyfriend, or if I even want him to be."

"I'm sorry, Kalli. I know that had to be frustrating. I hate it when Boomer doesn't listen to me."

"Exactly. So, I'm just going to have to prove to him I was onto something."

"And how do you plan to do that?"

"Chloe's neighbor has a security camera. She's a sweet little old lady, who I'm betting would love some of Ma's Mosaiko. I say we bring her some and have a cup of afternoon tea and dessert with her. She lives alone. I bet she would love the company."

"We?" Jaz groaned. "I promised Boomer I would stop letting you drag me along as your accomplice on your hairbrained schemes."

I gasped. "Excuse me. *You* were the one who dragged *me* to the strip club not long ago, if I'm not mistaken."

"Hey, I didn't say I agreed with him." Jaz laughed. "Our men can be so overprotective and difficult at times. That's why we have to stick together."

"And that's why I love you." I glanced at my phone then grabbed my purse and coat. "Let's go. Ma just texted me that the Mosaiko is ready."

"How'd you know I would say yes." Jaz quirked a brow.

"Because you love me, too." I blew her a kiss.

~

FIFTEEN MINUTES LATER, after a quick stop at Aphrodite's to pick up the Mosaiko and tea, Jaz and I were on our way to Chloe's neighbor's house. I parked down the street, far enough away that Chloe and Viggo wouldn't see my car. We got out and briskly walked to Gladys Leman's house.

I held the Mosaiko and tea while Jaz knocked on the door. I kept peeking over my shoulder, hoping Chloe or Viggo didn't look out their window and see me. I didn't need another reason for Nik to be mad at me without finding proof of something...anything...to help solve this case.

What felt like an eternity later, a little old lady with curlers in her thinning white hair answered the door. Faded blue eyes lit up as she spotted the goodies I had in my hand. "Well, land sakes, come in out of the cold, child." She held the door open wider. "You too, dear." She waved Jaz inside.

We entered, and she shut the door behind her. Jaz and I followed her to the kitchen table and shed several layers. It might be cold outside, but it felt like ninety in Gladys's house. Gladys filled a tea kettle with water, set it on the stove, and turned it on.

"I saw the tea in your hands. Won't you stay and have a cup?" She asked but didn't really leave us any option to do otherwise as she set cups, saucers, and plates on the table in front of three chairs.

This was perfect, as I needed time to execute my plan. I smiled wide. "Why, thank you, Gladys. That's so very kind of you."

"Oh, go on with you now. You're the kind one. I'd recognize your mama's Mosaiko anywhere. I'm honored you brought me some. To what do I owe this pleasure?" She sat down and waited for the kettle to boil.

"Chloe told me you'd been sick recently." That was actually the truth. "So, I asked Ma to make you some Mosaiko and tea."

"Well, aren't you the sweetest thing." The kettle whistled.

Jaz jumped up. "Allow me." She grabbed the kettle, turned the stove off, and poured water into our three cups.

I cut the Mosaiko and served us each a piece.

"Well, I don't know what to do with the two of you spoiling me like this. Since my Ernest passed, I haven't had anyone around to take care of me." She patted her curlers. "I mean, I can take care of myself, but it is lovely to have people stop by and do nice things for me. You two dears made my day."

"What about your children and grandchildren?" Jaz asked.

"They all live far away. I see them on holidays, and we Facetime, but I still get lonely. They did get me this fancy new security system." Gladys shook her head. "They set it all up, but I swear, I don't know how to use half of it."

"Let me take a look." This was perfect. Exactly what I needed. I would get information while I helped Gladys out. "I've been interested in getting one for my own house. Do you mind if I look through your footage? I can probably figure out how to use your system and make you a cheat sheet if that would help."

"Oh, could you, dear? That would be wonderful. And look away. I lead a pretty boring life. Not much happens on this street."

"Great. I'll get started while Jaz keeps you company."

Jaz raised a brow at me.

I jerked my head toward the living room.

"Yes, I would love to hear more about your family." Jaz stood and followed Gladys into the living room. "Do you have pictures you can show me?"

"Do I ever." Gladys walked over to an enormous bookshelf full of more photo albums than I'd ever seen in one person's home. "Follow me, dear. Let me start from the beginning." She was a sweet little old lady, but she was obviously obsessed with documenting every single aspect of her life over the years. And she had a lot of years.

Jaz shot me a look that said, *you owe me.*

I headed over to Gladys' computer and got to work. It didn't take long to figure out her system. My parents had the same system for their house and a much more advanced system for the restaurant. I brought up the security footage from Gladys' system and scrolled through hours' worth of footage from the night before, skimming quickly, making Gladys a cheat sheet as I went along.

Viggo was telling the truth.

He hadn't left the house all night long and no one showed up. Out of curiosity, I kept scrolling and looked at the day Viggo fell off the roof. I saw him climb up there and clear the roof just like he said. But then...

I sucked in a breath.

Jaz excused herself from Gladys, telling her she would be right back, as the woman looked for the next album. Jaz hurried over to my side and looked over my shoulder. "What's wrong? Did you find something?"

"Viggo was telling the truth about last night."

"Well, that's good. So why the gasp?"

"Because he was lying about something else." My gaze met hers. "Watch." I replayed the video for her.

Her jaw fell open and she winced. "Oh, my Lord, why would he do that?"

"Exactly." Viggo didn't fall off the roof and break his arm....

He jumped.

~

I KNOCKED on Nik's door later that night after I got home and changed into comfy yoga pants, fuzzy socks, and a soft fleece sweatshirt.

He didn't answer.

I sighed.

"I know you're in there, Nik. I heard you through the wall."

The door slowly opened, and he stepped back to let me inside. "I wasn't hiding. I just needed a minute."

I stared at him. "Well, maybe I needed a minute to explain why I was alone with Viggo, touching his arm."

He stared back silently.

I walked past him, took off my coat and boots, then carried my purse into his kitchen. He had takeout Chinese food he had just opened for dinner.

"You don't have to explain yourself to me." He followed me and sat down in a chair, popping the top to a beer.

"Apparently, I do." I opened a bottle of chardonnay and poured a glass then sat across from him.

"Have you eaten?" His eyes met mine.

I shook my head no, tucking my hair behind my ear. I'd left it down because I knew he liked it that way. "I haven't had much of an appetite lately."

"I have plenty of food if you're hungry now," he said softly.

I blinked. Were we really not going to talk about this?

He set his fork down and pushed his plate of food away. "Look, I wasn't mad at you, okay?"

"If that wasn't mad, then I'd hate to see you seriously angry."

"I mean, I *was* mad, but not at you. I was mad at the situation. It brought me right back to when my fiancée betrayed me. I never wanted to feel that way again, and I did for a moment. Then after I left, I knew immediately that I was being unfair to you in assuming you were anything like her."

"Thank you for that." I turned my glass on the table three times. "You're the only man I've ever said I love you to, and the only man I've ever wanted to. Our relationship is never going to work if you don't trust me."

His eyes turned tender. "I know. I love you, too. I'm sorry."

"Me, too." I reached out and slipped my hand into his.

*I missed you.* He smiled.

"Ditto." I smiled back. "So, I have news."

*Here we go.* Nik slipped his hand from mine and sat back, taking a sip of beer. "I'm listening."

"Want to know what I heard when I touched Viggo's arm?" I asked.

Nikos the Greek laughed harshly. "I'm not sure. Do I?"

"Yes, you definitely do." I left out the part where Viggo tried to take my coat off and assumed I couldn't get enough of him. "Viggo thought, and I quote, 'I can't go to jail, but Nikos will never help me if he knows the truth.'"

Detective Dreamy frowned. "The truth about what?"

"I'm not sure. I have a feeling he's told a few lies, but I did discover something I think you'll find very interesting."

"You mean when you were *not* investigating Delilah's murder?" He raised a brow at me and took another sip of his beer.

"Actually, I wasn't investigating her murder." I bit my bottom lip and paused a moment to sip my chardonnay. "I was investigating Mack's."

"How? I was at the crime scene all afternoon, talking to Theresa, and you never showed up."

"That doesn't mean I wasn't following a lead."

"Okay, I'll bite."

"Well, we all know Mack and Viggo almost fought at the pawn shop. Then Viggo didn't go to the Winter Carnival. He said he went home. Your Ma never went home. She spent the night at the captains, and—"

Nik held his hand up. "I don't need to hear about that part." He opened another beer and took a drink.

"—and Viggo says he stayed in. Or so he thinks. He said he had too much to drink. I saw the beer bottles on the counter. He's a big guy. It would take a lot more than that to make him forget the evening."

"Agreed. So, what did you do?"

"Well, after hearing Viggo's thoughts, I knew I needed proof that he stayed home on the night of Mack's murder."

"And did you find any?"

"I noticed your Ma's neighbor, Gladys Leman, has security cameras on the outside of her house. So, I—"

"Bothered poor Gladys." Nik shook his head. "Why didn't you call me instead? It's my job."

"Because *someone* wasn't talking to me." I pointed my finger at him.

"That poor little old lady lives alone. She doesn't need people bothering her." He pointed back. "She can sue you for harassment, you know."

"I wasn't harassing her. I know she lives alone. I also know she wasn't feeling well recently. So, I had Ma make some Mosaiko for her, and Jaz and I—"

"You got Jaz involved?" Nik ran a hand over his face, looking tired. "Boomer's not going to like that."

"Are you going to keep interrupting me, or are you going to let me finish my story?" I strummed my fingers on the table.

Nik held his hands up and motioned for me to continue.

"Gladys loved the company; I'll have you know. She showed Jaz all of her photo albums while I made a cheat sheet for her on how to use her security camera. I asked permission if I could make a copy of a few nights of footage, and she didn't mind one bit. She wants these murders solved as much as everyone else does."

"I take it you found something interesting?"

I pulled a thumb drive out of my purse and set it on the table. "Viggo was telling the truth about staying home the night of Mack's murder."

"Well, that's good at least."

"There's more."

"Like what?"

"He was definitely lying about something else." I tossed a wink in Detective Dreamy's direction, letting him know I held some pretty important cards in this investigation.

"Why doesn't that surprise me? What has my cousin done now?"

"Well," I took a page out of Ma's book and paused in dramatic fashion before dropping the bomb, "he didn't fall off your ma's roof, for one."

Nik's brows drew together. "Then how did he break his arm and crack his ribs?"

"He jumped off the roof."

Nik gaped at me. "You're sure?"

"See for yourself."

Nik went and got his laptop then fired it up and plugged in the thumb drive. "This doesn't make any sense. Why in all of Mount Olympus would anyone want to jump off a roof." He looked at me and his eyes widened with obvious concern. "Unless they were trying to kill themselves?"

"I don't think so. Look at the footage again. I saw this documentary once on stunt doubles. Viggo fell exactly like they did to be sure he wouldn't die. But why would he want to hurt himself?"

"I don't know," Nik clenched his jaw, "but you can bet I'm going to find out."

## 13

The next morning, Nik headed to his ma's house to talk to Viggo, while I headed to the Winter Carnival at the park. Jaz and I were manning our booth. I carried our breakfast order from the Sinfully Delicious tent down Restaurant Row to the shopping section on Looter's Lane.

I waved to Dixie in her Doolittle's Doodads booth, but she didn't see me. She seemed distracted, but there wasn't anyone at her booth yet. She kept looking around almost nervously. I mentally filed that note away.

Meanwhile, Theresa looked calm and...happy... smiling and greeting everyone who walked by. You would never know her husband was just murdered. Then again, she was free from abuse now.

Abuse for years could make *any* person capable of murder. I'd heard about the Domestic Violence Survivor's Justice Act, specifically established to protect abused women after saving themselves in whatever way they had to.

Maybe Mack confronted Theresa at her shop, and she was prepared with a knife this time.

"What are you thinking so hard on?" Jaz asked curiously as I entered our booth.

"Murder and what it might take to push a woman to that."

"Ah, are you and Detective Dreamy still fighting?"

I laughed. "Good Lord, this isn't about us. We made up, but he wasn't happy I meddled in his case again, though."

Jaz shook her head. "Neither was Boomer."

"Well, this time I did actually drag you with me." I winced. "Sorry."

"You have nothing to be sorry about. I told him I am a strong, independent woman who can make up my own mind on what I can or can't do."

"Even though we might have disagreements with our men, neither one of us would want to see them dead." I glanced over at a smiling Theresa as she waited on customers. "But I'm not so sure someone else felt that way about *her* man."

Jaz followed my eyes. "I can't say that I would blame her if she did murder her husband. It could easily have been self-defense if he was hitting her."

"That's true, but then why try to hide it? Nik said she claims she hadn't seen Mack since his argument with Viggo outside her shop. She went to the carnival that night to run her booth, and then went home. She said he never came home that night. Leonard the maintenance man found him in the dumpster the next morning as he was waiting to meet her to do some work on her shop."

"Yeah, but even if it was self-defense, she could have freaked out and tried to cover it up, claiming it was someone else."

"Does she look freaked out to you?" I raised a brow.

Jaz crossed her arms. "Not one bit." She raised a hand to shield her eyes and looked closer. "Hey, is that...?"

"Oh, no," I said. "It certainly is."

Viggo stepped up to Finley's Finds and set something on the counter. I could only guess, but I was betting it was his grandfather's watch. Why was he so desperate to sell it? Theresa was studying it when another man joined them. My jaw fell open. It was the tall, suave, silver fox who was with Knox at Flannigan's Pub.

Viggo looked like he didn't know the man. The man started talking to him, and I could see Viggo's face turn red from way over here. He said something back, then took the pocket watch back from Theresa and walked angrily away. The man spoke to Theresa for a moment, then he walked away, following Viggo from a distance.

I sent a text to Nik with what I'd just seen. "Hey, I'm going to talk to Theresa. Can you watch my designs?"

"Of course." Jaz stepped away to wait on a customer.

Tightening my coat against the chill, I walked over to Theresa's booth.

"Hi, Theresa, how are you doing?" I smiled with sympathy.

"I'm great," she said and sounded sincere. "I know it sounds horrible, but I'm glad Mack's gone. He wasn't a nice man. He hurt me...a lot." She took a deep breath. "But he won't ever hurt me again."

"I'm so sorry you had to go through that. No man or woman should ever have to go through mental or physical abuse. Are you going to be okay on your own?" I reached out and touched her arm.

*I hated him. He deserved everything he got.* Theresa patted my hand then stepped away. "I started my business years ago so I would be self-sufficient and could leave him. I tried once, but he beat me so bad, I had to stay in bed for days." She let out a harsh laugh and hugged herself. "He told everyone I had the flu. I never tried again. I figured he would kill me the next time." Her eyes met mine. "The only way I could be free was if he died."

"You know, if he was hitting you, you had the right to defend yourself." I watched her carefully.

Her eyes widened. "Honey, I didn't kill him. Not that I wouldn't have if I'd had the chance, but the truth is, I didn't do it." She shook her head. "I don't know who did kill him, but I'm grateful just the same. Mack might have been mean, but he was smart with money. I'll be set for life, and I'll never marry again."

"I get it." I nodded. "Hey, I saw a man talking to Viggo a little while ago. Do you have any idea who he is?"

"I have no idea. I've never seen him around town before."

"It looked like Viggo didn't know him, either, but then it looked like the man might have said something that upset Viggo. Did you happen to hear what it was?"

She thought about it for a minute. "He said something about you don't have a choice. You *will* do this or there will be consequences."

"Oh, wow. How did Viggo respond to that?"

"Not well. He was pretty angry. Viggo said something about not letting anyone control him anymore." She held up her hands. "I stayed out of it because I know all too well how it feels to be controlled."

The wind swirled a flurry of snow through the air around us.

I tightened my coat. "He didn't say anything about his fellow models, Zelda and Knox, did he?"

Theresa shrugged. "Nothing to me." Some shoppers stopped in and were looking at her display cases.

"Thanks, Theresa. You've been a big help." I didn't want to keep her if she had to get back to work. I waved and started to leave.

She smiled and nodded as she headed over to the customers, but then stopped short and turned back to me. "Hey, Kalli, you don't think Viggo killed Mack, do you?"

"No, he was home all night. I have security footage to prove it. Now we just have to find a way to prove he didn't kill Delilah."

"Good luck."

"Thanks."

I walked away, thinking about what the silver fox stranger had said to Viggo. Viggo had looked like he didn't recognize the man. If he had been from the modeling agency, Viggo would have recognized him for sure. If he wasn't with the modeling agency, then who on earth did he work for?

*Oh, Viggo, your cuz is not going to be happy with you. What have you gotten yourself involved in this time?*

~

AT LUNCH, I walked over to Restaurant Row with an order for Jaz and me from Diner Delights. My cousins' deli was right next door to Vincenzo's booth. As long as I wasn't eating at the Italian restaurant, Ma wasn't mad. My whole family supported each other, so eating at my cousins' deli was a given.

Fraternizing with the enemy, however, was not allowed.

Ma and Vinny competed in everything, driving everyone crazy. Things used to get really bad between them, but they had formed a truce of sorts. The truce had held up for a while now, much to everyone's surprise.

I walked up to the counter of Diner Delights, and Aunt Tasoula was there, placing her own order.

"Ah, Kalliope. Good. You eat."

"I eat every day, Aunt Tasoula."

"You too skinny. You man no like skinny. Men like curves. Like me." She popped a hip and tapped it.

"I'll keep that in mind." I laughed.

"Big curves help you make big babies." She wagged her eyebrows.

"I'm pretty sure that's not how it works." I felt the blood drain from my face just thinking about babies, big or otherwise, growing in my body. I was terrified of what it would do to my insides.

Nik and I weren't engaged or anything. We had only just become official and weren't even living together yet. Still...babies were something we'd never discussed. I didn't even know if he wanted children. I didn't know if he wanted marriage, either. I was only just getting to know the other side of his family.

I suddenly realized there was a lot I didn't know about Nikos Stevens.

I tried not to get in my head about it. It didn't matter what pace others were going at. Nik and I were forging ahead at our own pace. He understood my quirks and what it meant to date someone like me, and yet he was still here. That had to be a good sign. For once, I had high hopes for my future.

All of a sudden, there was shouting coming from Vinny's restaurant next door.

"Oh, no." A premonition of doom filled me.

"Oh, yes," Aunt Tasoula said gravely. "It's the goblins again."

"Hold that food, Kosmos," I said.

"You got it." He set our orders under the warmer.

Aunt Tasoula and I ran over to the booth next door.

"What are you doing, you crazy Greek mama?" Vinnywas swinging his hands through the air, trying to catch Ma's spatula as it whacked plate after plate of pasta, waiting to be sauced.

"I no crazy. I trying to save you."

"From what?"

"Kolovelonis!"

"I don't know a Kolo whatever." He waved his apron in the air. "All I know is you are ruining my macaroni."

"It's no macaroni." Ma's beehive, encased in the largest hairnet they made, swayed from side-to-side as she talked....more like ranted. "Kolovelonis look like a skinny string of macaroni, but he sneaky. He squeeze through your colander and make mischief. You'll see."

"The only one who is making mischief is you. Go!" He pointed at her. "Make mischief at your own restaurant. All these people waiting for their lunch, and you ruined their meals. You're just jealous because my chili beat yours in the cookoff. Yours wasn't spicy enough. You're trying to ruin *me*. Our truce is over."

"I knew you too good to be trusted." Ma swiped her spatula through the air in the shape of an X. "You no appreciate the Greeks. Fine! But you no blame me when the goblins make a mess."

"Goblins?" Vinny scratched his head. "You really

*are* crazy."

"You really *gonna* be sorry. You want spicy? I show you spicy!" Ma let loose a string of curse words in Greek and stormed off, batting imaginary goblins along the way. What *sorry* meant was anyone's guess. But one thing was certain...

Mischievous goblins were the least of his worries.

"I'M REALLY WORRIED," Chloe said to Nik that evening at the carnival.

Captain Crenshaw had left to get them some dinner. My shift had ended, and we were at the ice-skating rink in the park that had been constructed just for the Winter Carnival. The couples' competition just ended, and the free skate was starting.

"Why are you worried?" I asked her.

"Viggo hasn't been home all day."

"I think he's avoiding me," Nik said. "I've been looking for him all day to confront him about jumping off your roof. And then, after Kalli texted me earlier about some stranger threatening him if he didn't do something, and Viggo saying he was sick of being controlled, I called him." Nik looked at his ma. "He didn't answer."

"What do you think it means?" Chloe asked.

"That he's hiding something."

"Who's hiding something?" Captain Crenshaw carried two plates from Rosalita's Restaurant and handed one to Chloe.

"Don't tell your ma." Chloe winked at me.

"Don't worry. I love Mexican food, too. And after her truce with Vinnyended in disaster, I'm not saying a word."

"Viggo is hiding something. I know my cousin, and I would bet my badge on it." Nik filled the captain in on everything he'd just told his ma. "I'd like to find out more about this stranger. He's the key."

"Agreed. I'll put him on everyone's radar. We'll get to the bottom of this." The captain stepped aside and made a phone call.

"Oh, look! Eleni's up. Come on." I walked over to the edge of the rink to watch my cousin Eleni compete in the free style skate event with the rest of our families. Eleni had been figure skating her whole life and was really good.

All of my family and Nik's were there, with the exception of Viggo. Eleni skated to the movie *Frozen's* soundtrack, getting the crowd all fired up as she did spins and jumps and landed a triple axel.

Frona ran around, singing, "Let it go," while releasing the helium balloons placed strategically around the rink.

YiaYia caught a couple but not many.

Aunt Tasoula whipped her coat off, shouting, "The cold never bothered me anyway. Not with the mamapause." She fanned her face.

"It's menopause, 'Soula." Ma shook her head.

Aunt Tasoula shrugged. "That's what I say. It pause me from being a mama. So, I call it mamapause." She nodded once.

"That no mean you not a *mama*." Ma stabbed a finger at her with a mischievous grin. "And a *grandmama*."

"Bite your tongue." Aunt Tasoula raised her chin a notch and patted her chest. "You right. I am a pretty grand mama, but I no *Grandmama*. I G-ma."

"You something." Ma grunted.

The crowd cheered when they announced that

Eleni had won. My family all went off to celebrate, and we were about to join them when suddenly I spotted Sherry, Bennett, Yvonne, and Humphry across the rink. I squinted to see them better.

"You coming?" Nik looking at me.

"Yeah, just a minute, though." I pointed across the rink. "Look who's here."

Nik's gaze followed mine. "Oh, that's nice, but not surprising. They've been attending all the Winter Carnival events."

"True but take a closer look. Either Bennett has started wearing eye shadow, or he has one big shiner."

Nik studied him. "You're right. I don't know what's happening around here lately, but Clearview seems to be falling apart." He started heading in their direction.

"What are you doing?" I jogged after him.

"My duty." He looked at me over his shoulder. "He's a guest in our town. The least I can do is see if he's okay."

"Ladies." Nik tipped his head to Sherry and Yvonne, then turned to Bennett and Humphry. "Gentlemen."

"Detective Stevens, right?" Humphry held out his hand with a smile.

"That's right." Nik shook his hand. "I hope our town is treating you well."

"The people here seem really nice." Humphry's gaze shot to me briefly, before settling on Yvonne.

"The town's okay." She shrugged. "My tastes run a little fancier."

"I love this town, but it seems to be getting dangerous." Sherry gave her husband a pointed look.

He sighed and shook his head. "I told you it was nothing, dear."

"I wouldn't call a black eye nothing, *dear*."

"May I ask what happened?" Nik studied Bennett.

"I was having a cigar in the smoking section of the park at dusk last night. When I finished, I started walking back to find Sherry, but I couldn't see that well. I tripped over a stump and hit my head on a bench. That's all."

"That's enough." She placed her hands on his cheeks, looking genuinely distressed. "You could have lost an eye."

"You worry too much, darling." Bennett took her hands in his own and kissed each one, then hugged her.

"I can assure you Clearview Police Department is doing all it can to keep our town safe. I can talk to the mayor about installing more lights over there, especially during our winter festivals. It gets dark so early this time of year."

"I really appreciate that," Sherry said. "Thank you so much, Detective."

"My pleasure," Nik said when his phone rang. "Excuse me a minute." He answered, "Detective Stevens here." His brows drew together. "When did this happen?" He nodded. "I'm on my way." He hung up.

"What's wrong?" I asked, not having a good feeling in the pit of my stomach.

"Doolittle's Doodads has been robbed."

Humphry and Bennett looked at each other with wide eyes, while Sherry gasped, and Yvonne shook her head with a frown of displeasure. If Clearview didn't get a handle on all this crime, we wouldn't have any tourists left. No one said it, but it was obvious from their expressions they were all thinking one thing...

Clearview Police Department obviously wasn't doing enough.

**14**

S unday brunch was held inside since it was winter. We usually took turns between the Pagonis and Ballas families. My parents' house was the biggest, and with my cousins all finding love—except for Yanni, Thalia, and Eleni—the families were growing.

My parents had a two-story colonial with fountains and statues out front as well as out back and a gazebo with lights, which was covered with snow at the moment. Inside, everyone congregated in the great room and open kitchen. The island was full of breakfast and lunch Greek foods set up buffet style.

Kosmos and Winnie were talking and laughing with Silas and Zena as they filled their plates. YiaYia and Papou were dancing in the living room with Aunt Tasoula and Tate, while Eleni took a turn corralling Frona. Ma and Pop were talking with Father Papadopoulos and Jasper about his adoption and getting him baptized in the church. While Nik was near the sunroom talking to Captain Crenshaw, Chloe, and Viggo.

I refilled the punch bowl as Jaz and Boomer walked through the door.

Boomer eyed the island. "Oh, yes. I was hoping your mother would make her chicken kababs with Tzatziki sauce. Those are so good."

"Well, there's plenty of that and everything else. Greek mamas never let you or anyone go hungry."

"That's what I love about Sunday brunch." He rubbed his hands together and grabbed a plate. Within minutes, he finished his food as Jaz and I watched him in awed silence, then he refilled his plate with a wink at Jaz before heading over to join Nik and the captain.

"Wow," was all I said.

"Yeah." Jaz laughed. "It's scary cooking for that one. And he never gains an ounce." She shook her head.

"You could be talking about yourself right now." I laughed.

"True. I do love to eat."

"I can't imagine what your kids will be like."

Her face paled. "I hadn't thought of that. Good Lord, I'm going to need to hire a chef." She patted her cheeks until they regained color. "First things first. If I survive planning this wedding, it will be a miracle."

"You'll do great. I'm sure that, whatever you decide on, it will be an amazing wedding. You have great taste."

"Awe, thanks." She hugged me. *Speaking of weddings...*

"As you said, first things first." I sighed, glancing over at Nik. "I realized the other day that I don't even know if he wants children." I shivered, wrapping my arms around my middle. "I don't even know if *I* want children. I'm not so sure I can handle having a human being growing inside me. The thought of my organs moving around to make room for a watermelon and then giving birth to that terrifies me." I looked my best friend in the eyes, feeling my anxiety creeping in. "What if Nik thinks I'm a horrible person because of that?"

"Nik adores you, but you're right. Marriage is a big step. These are conversations you need to have before even thinking about spending your lives together."

"Luckily, he's only asked to knock down a wall." I shrugged. "Who knows if he'll ever propose."

"That's true," she said gently, "but you still need to figure out what you want. What will make you happy?"

"I really don't know." My gaze wandered around the room at my family. They all seemed to know exactly what they wanted. I blinked. "When did Yanni and Thalia get here? And why on earth did they bring Parker and Claudett?"

Jaz looked over at the two couples who were deep in conversation by the fireplace. "Good question. I didn't realize Parker and Yanni were friends."

"Nik says they're spending a lot of time together at the gym. I know Thalia is looking for a house for him, and Yanni might just be designing his landscaping. As for Claudett, I have no idea why she's Yanni's plus one."

"Well, she *is* a temp," Jaz said. "I heard Delilah's business went to Andrew, and then he sold it to Cameron."

"Yeah, I saw her at the bank. And then Dixie came storming in. She wasn't happy about Andrew being the beneficiary. Delilah had taken out a big life insurance policy just before she died. Dixie hired a lawyer."

"Oh, wow, I hadn't heard that." Jaz frowned. "Do you think Andrew could have killed Delilah if he knew about the policy? I mean, she didn't get back with him. Hooking up with Viggo could have pushed Andrew over the edge."

"That's a possibility," I agreed.

"Or Dixie could have killed her sister," Jaz pointed out.

"They did have a fight the day before she died. Maybe she never went to NYC at all. Nik said there was no record of her at the hotel she claimed to have stayed at."

"I can't imagine any fight that could push me to kill my sister, let alone a twin." Jaz shook her head. "I really hope that's not the case. That would be so sad. What's also sad is Cameron not keeping Claudett on permanently."

"Hmmm, Yanni did lose his assistant recently. I wonder if he hired Claudett? But why bring her as a plus one? He's usually all business."

"Maybe Claudett isn't just business to him."

"Maybe." I studied Claudett with newfound interest and hope.

"I know Parker is definitely not just business for Thalia," Jaz pointed out.

My smile slipped into a frown. "Now that's a relationship I *don't* want to see thrive. I don't trust the guy."

Jaz nodded. "I don't trust Cameron. I saw her at Sinfully Delicious having coffee with Roman yesterday morning."

"Nik and I saw Cameron with Roman the other night," I said. "What do you think that means?"

"I don't have any idea. Not long ago, he was her boss's rival. You would think she wouldn't want anything to do with the man. Who's to say he didn't kill Delilah to take out his competition?"

"There are so many suspects. We need to start narrowing them down soon if Viggo is going to have a chance of staying free," I said as Nik and Boomer came over to join us. "Any updates?"

"Viggo's not talking." Nik rubbed his jaw. "He won't open up about who that stranger is and what he's trying to make Viggo do. He claims he's with his agency and just trying to make him come back to work."

"Do you believe him?" I glanced over to Viggo who was still talking to Chloe and the captain. He seemed agitated, and then he walked out.

"I'm not sure." Nik sighed. "Something seems off with him. I've never seen him so fidgety and nervous. I'm going to talk to Zelda and Knox. Maybe they'll have more answers than him."

"Well, I did see Knox with that man at the Winter Carnival, so maybe he really is with the agency," I said.

"Maybe," Boomer added, "but I don't get how they're controlling him. I'm going to look into the agency itself."

"Hey, did either of you ever find any answers on who broke into Dixie's shop?" Jaz looked at both Boomer and Nik.

"No, but something's off there as well," Boomer responded.

"I agree." Nik nodded. "She did ask me if something of value was found in an item that was legitimately purchased, does it have to be given back to the original owner."

"Interesting," Boomer said. "She claims the perpetrator didn't take anything. Why would the person break in and trash the place but not take anything?"

"Maybe whoever killed Delilah didn't follow her for something they thought *she* had," Nik said. "Maybe they were after something they think *Dixie* has. It was her house, after all, and now this is her shop."

"Either way," Boomer looked both Jaz and me in the eyes, "you ladies lock your doors. There's still a killer on the loose, and apparently, he or she is still in town and not finished with whatever they're after."

AFTER BRUNCH, I headed over to Doolittle's Doodads. I wanted to see the damage for myself. And see if I could find out any more on what she *wasn't* saying. I walked up to the front door, and the window was boarded up. The sign still said open, but there was no glass left in the windowpane.

I opened the door and went inside.

Dixie looked up with a smile on her face...until she saw me. "Oh, it's you. I already answered all of your boyfriend's questions."

"I'm not here about that." I walked over to the front desk, carrying a potted plant from Yanni's Yards. "No dessert this time." I grinned.

Dixie didn't.

"Look, I think we got off on the wrong foot, and I wanted to start over," I said. "My cousin Yanni said you like plants, so I thought I would buy you one for your shop as a peace offering." I held the plant out to her.

She took it reluctantly and set it on the counter. "Thank you."

"Yanni said that a Bromeliad Guzmania house-plant was the perfect choice. It would brighten up your shop, adding color. They maintain their color for many weeks with little to no effort. I think the long, narrow, shiny green leaves with the large, showy flower in the center is so pretty, don't you?"

"I'm familiar with Guzmania plants. They're lovely, and they aren't difficult bromeliads to grow. Thank you for this. I really do appreciate it. At least one good thing has happened lately. Good thing they don't require much light." She glanced toward her broken window.

"I saw your window is broken. That's terrible." I looked around, genuinely feeling bad for her. I knew how much work went into starting and running your own business. "Did the thief do much damage to your antiques?"

"No. A few shelves were turned over and drawers upended, but nothing was stolen." She shrugged, looking around warily.

"Do you think someone was looking for something specific?"

Her gaze snapped up to mine. "Why would you ask that?"

"I mean, first your house and now this. I'm so sorry this happened to you." I reached out and squeezed her arm. "I'm really worried about you."

*You and me both after that threatening note.* She just smiled and tilted her head once but didn't say anything.

"Is that why you went to NYC on New Year's Eve? To run away from something...or someone?" I asked, injecting sincerity into my voice. "Although, your name wasn't on the list at the hotel you said you stayed at."

She moved her arm away from mine. "I used an alias."

"Why? Is someone after you, Dixie? The police can help protect you, but you have to be honest with them."

She took a deep breath but then cleared her

throat. "I don't know what you're talking about. I think your boyfriend is rubbing off on you. Many people in my line of work use an alias so our competition doesn't get wind of any tips on some fabulous finds. The last thing any of us wants is a bidding war."

"I see." I handed her my business card. "If you ever need anything at all, even just someone to talk to, I'm just a phone call away."

She took the card. "Thank you." I started to walk away and then looked over my shoulder as I opened the door. "Dixie?"

She looked up. "Yes?"

"Take care of yourself. There's still a killer on the loose out there."

She paused a moment and looked at me. "I will. Thanks again for the plant, Kalli." She gave me the first sincere smile since I'd met her.

"You're very welcome." I smiled back and then walked out the door, closing it behind me, without looking ahead. A moment later, I ran smack dab into Leonard Murphy the maintenance man.

He reached out and grabbed my arms to steady me. *Jeesh, lady. Watch where you're going or you're gonna get hurt.*

"I'm fine," I said a little startled.

"Excuse me?" He pushed his glasses up his freckled nose, looking confused as his pale cheeks flushed.

*Whoops.* I sometimes forgot when I heard a thought, that it wasn't spoken out loud. "I just wanted to reassure you that I was fine, in case you were wondering. I should have been watching where I was going."

"Ah, that's funny. It's like you read my mind or

something." He cleared his throat. "Are you sure you're okay? We collided pretty hard."

"Yes, I'm okay." I smiled reassuringly. "Are you here on a job?"

He nodded. "Yes, actually. I know I'm pretty new to town, but the folks around here sure are keeping me busy lately."

"I can only imagine. Power outages, break-ins... dead bodies in dumpsters. You've certainly had quite the experience so far."

I didn't know Leonard that well. We'd only spoken a few times when he did work for my parents at the restaurant. He seemed like a nice enough guy, and he was very good at his job. He could fix literally anything.

"Yeah, seeing a dead body is no fun." He shoved his hands in his jeans.

"I'm familiar with the feeling," I said sympathetically. "You got to Finley's Finds before Mrs. Finley, didn't you?"

He nodded. "The store wasn't open yet, but I hate being late." He looked off as if pondering something and said more to himself, "If only the door hadn't been cracked open, I never would have set out to investigate."

"Wait, the door was open?" I blinked. "That wasn't in the police report." I definitely would have remembered that detail.

His face flushed a deeper red as he held up his hands. "Look, I just want out of this. I wasn't supposed to say anything."

"Who told you not to say anything?"

"Mrs. Finley."

My lips parted. *Well, that was unexpected.* This case just kept getting more and more interesting. "If you have any information that can help solve this murder, then I think it's important to say everything, don't you?"

He seemed to ponder that for a moment, then he sighed. "When I got there, the door was cracked open. I peeked inside, but everything looked fine. I looked around the building to see if I could see anyone or any clues."

"Really? I'm surprised you didn't call the police right away."

"I wasn't sure what exactly had happened. I guess it was just instinct to walk around the building and make sure it was clear." He shrugged. "I watch a lot of cop shows." He half grinned. "Anyway, when I was out back, I saw someone's hat on the ground. I guess that's what made me look in the dumpster. I never expected to see Mr. Finley dead inside." He shuddered. "*That* was when I called the police. Mrs. Finley showed up just as I hung up."

"Why would she tell you not to say anything? That doesn't make any sense." I watched him closely.

"She said nothing was missing. Maybe she forgot to lock up. She just wanted everyone to stay out of her business, and she couldn't afford for her shop to become a crime scene. I figured, if nothing was missing, then what was the harm?"

"Do you think Mack was the one who opened the door?"

"I don't know what to think, ma'am."

"Please, call me Kalli."

"If Mr. Finley was snooping in his wife's business, then that's between them. If he stabbed himself, the knife would still be there. Maybe someone else was in the shop, snooping around or waiting for her, and he caught them in the act. The perpetrator could have killed him and then took off."

"What about her security camera?"

He snorted. "That was what I was there to fix."

"Well, thank you for being honest with me, Mr. Murphy."

"It's Leonard." He tipped his head. "If that's all, I have work to do."

I waved goodbye and walked away, wondering why Theresa's door had been open. Was her security camera really broken, or did someone tamper with it to do some snooping? Her lock hadn't been broken, so how did the person get inside? Was it someone she knew? Did she give them a key?

What exactly was Theresa Finley hiding?

## 15

Later that afternoon, I knocked on Jaz's apartment door after her frantic call. The door whipped open to a teary-eyed Jaz. Her hair was in a messy bun, her lounge pants and sweatshirt mismatched, and her face make-up free.

It really was a crisis.

"What is going on?" She'd called asking me to come over right away then she hung up. Looking at her now, I was worried she and Boomer broke up because I couldn't imagine anything else that would have her this upset.

"Chanel and Versace are gone!" she wailed.

I stood corrected. Her babies were everything to her.

"Okay, let me come in, and we'll figure this out."

She stood back and held the door open. I stepped inside, noticing all the feminine touches she had added to Boomer's bachelor pad. All the dog beds and toys were still there. I walked to the kitchen and poured her a glass of water. After she sat on the couch and took a drink, I sat down next to her.

"Start from the beginning, and don't leave anything out."

"The dogs were fine this morning. Completely fine. Boomer and I got them all tired out and settled before we went to Sunday brunch at your ma's house. I finally talked him into doing some wedding shopping with me. We were gone all afternoon, but the dogs sleep a lot during the day, so we knew they would be fine." She started crying again. "They're not fine. They gone. Out in the big, bad world all alone."

"Pull yourself together, Mama." I waited while she composed herself. "So you came home, and what happened next?"

"Boomer dropped me off because Nik had called him and wanted his help following a new lead. So, I let myself into our apartment and searched everywhere. I thought maybe they were hiding, but they weren't anywhere to be found."

"They couldn't have just disappeared," I said logically, running all sorts of possibilities through my brain.

"That's what I thought, so I went running up and down the hall, looking for them. Several people said they complained because of all the barking."

"But your girls are always so well-behaved." I was shocked. Were we talking about the same dogs? "They *never* bark."

"Exactly. Although, lately, they have been acting out of sorts. Definitely not their normal selves. I have an appointment at the vet tomorrow to see what's going on."

"Did you talk to your landlord?"

"I tried, but she's not in. Although, I did have a missed call from her earlier. Probably about the barking."

"Did you call Boomer?"

"No, I called you. I know he's working, and I didn't want to upset him. We need to find them, Kalli."

"Let's assume they got out somehow. Let's go check out their favorite places and see if they're there." I stood up and grabbed my coat.

"Okay, yes. I will feel better doing something. I can't just sit here anymore." She grabbed her coat and followed me.

First, we went to Dino's Doggy Daycare with no luck. Then we went to the animal shelter, and they hadn't seen them. Next up was the Winter Carnival with all the food trucks and the fenced-in dog park. No one had seen them there, either.

We drove down every street in Clearview, but still no luck. None of the store owners had seen them. We showed a bunch of tourists their picture, but again, no one had seen them. Chanel and Versace were full-sized gorgeous black poodles.

They were kind of hard to miss.

"I just don't understand. How could they have literally vanished into thin air?" Jaz wrung her hands together.

Suddenly we saw Milly Donovan the dog walker walking around frantically, calling down alleyways and streets. I pulled over and Jaz rolled down the window to my Prius. We both gasped. Milly was calling for Chanel and Versace. We both flew out of my car at the same time and flagged Milly down.

She was out of breath and pale when she reached us. "I'm so sorry, Jaz. I feel horrible." Her voice wobbled and her hands shook.

Jaz was suddenly the calm one, in mom mode. "It's okay, Milly, just calm down and take a deep breath." When the woman complied, she continued. "Why are you calling for my dogs? Have you seen them?"

Milly bit her bottom lip and nodded her head yes. "I thought today was my day to walk them, so I used the spare key you gave me and picked them up."

Jaz had Milly walk the dogs several times a week when she was at work, but she'd taken today off last minute and cancelled so she could attend Sunday brunch and wedding shop with Boomer. "It's my fault. I cancelled last minute." Jaz tended to ramble when she was upset. "I didn't want to pass up a chance to shop with Boomer since he had a free afternoon. We walked them early before we left for brunch and shopping."

"I get it. That is how I was when Nelson and I were planning our wedding. Now that I'm pregnant, my brain is mush."

"Congratulations," I said, happy for them, but still concerned for Jaz, "but what happened to the dogs after you picked them up?"

"Well, I had barely started our walk, when the girls started frantically barking and then took off. I tried to hold onto their leashes, but they were too strong for me. I've never seen them behave this way before. It was definitely out of character for them."

"Why didn't you call me?" Jaz asked.

"I was so upset. I've been searching for hours." Milly's voice wobbled again, and her eyes filled up with tears. "If anything happens to them, I will be devastated. It's getting dark so early still."

I was proud of Jaz. She held it together for Milly's sake.

"Nothing is going to happen to them. My girls are tough. I'm going to make up flyers and let everyone know to be on the lookout."

"Can we give you a lift home?" I asked.

"No, I'll just stop into the jewelry store. Nelson is waiting for me. Please keep me posted."

"We will," I said.

Jaz climbed into the car without another word.

I dropped Jaz off at her apartment to get started on the flyers, and then I went home, keeping my eyes peeled along the way. It was dusk and dinnertime now as I pulled into our driveway. Nik hadn't gotten home yet. I went inside my house first, to feed Ms. Priss and change my clothes. Then, I headed next door to feed Wolfgang.

I opened the door and my jaw hit the floor.

Nik always kept the sliding door cracked for Wolf because he liked the fresh air. The Saint Bernard had pushed the door wide open. He'd only done that once before, when he broke through our fence to protect me. Why on earth had he done that this time? I walked over to the sliding door and looked outside. There was a big hole under the fence. Closing the door, I turned around and couldn't believe my eyes.

Wolfgang lay sprawled out on the floor with Chanel and Versace on both sides of him.

I felt like I'd walking into a frat house the morning after a raging party and suddenly knew what it must feel like to be a parent. I had a suspicious feeling why the girls had been acting so crazy lately.

I called Jaz and she picked up on the first ring.

"Did you find them?" she asked.

"Oh, I found them, all right."

"Where?"

"In Nik's apartment with a very satisfied looking naughty boy."

"What does that mean?"

"He's a purebred Saint Bernard and they are purebred Poodles, and none of them are spayed or neutered."

"Right…so?"

"So, if I'm not mistaken, your girls were in heat. Your life is going to get a whole lot busier in about two months with a whole pack of Saint Berdoodles."

A gasp followed by a loud clunk happened seconds before the line went dead.

~

"WHY DO you need me to go with you, Ma?" I asked my mother when she picked me up on my lunch break to go to Cromwell's Creations.

Roman Cromwell considered himself to be the best party planner who created the most fabulous events of all kinds. Since no one knew for sure what Cameron planned to do with Delilah's business once she bought it from Andrew, Roman was the only game in town at the moment.

"To support you new brother," Ma said, nodding her head once.

"Ma, he's been my brother since the day he was born," I pointed out logically. "I just didn't know it."

"Ah, but he's a *new* Ballas." Her face transformed into one of happiness. "I finally have my baby boy."

"He's twenty-seven, Ma. He's hardly a baby," I grumbled, not sure why this was bothering me.

Her eyes shot over to me and then back at the road. "Ah, the green-eyed monster got you."

I gaped. "I am not jealous." *Was I?*

I was happy I'd met Jasper, and I wanted him in my life. I just hadn't thought he would be in my family. I felt horrible even thinking that, but I was used to being an only child. My family might be crazy, but they were mine.

"You will always be my first baby, Kalliope. Because of you, I became a mom," Ma said softly. "Never forget that."

"I know, it's silly to be jealous. I got lucky. Jasper didn't. Our lives could very easily have been the other way around. I want him as part of our family. I just don't want you to love him more."

"I big mama." She patted her ample bosom. "I have lots of love. You see. I be a good mama."

"You're the *best* mama." I reached over and squeezed her hand.

*Oh, my Kalliope, you gonna make me ugly cry and ruin my face.*

I let go of her hand. "Your face could never be ugly, Ma."

She looked at me with big eyes then tapped her head, shaking it hard.

"Ma, what are you doing?"

"I shake out that goblin. He crawl in my brain and whisper in you ear." She pointed her finger at me as she pulled into the parking lot. "You no listen to him."

I bit back a grin. "No worries, Ma. I'll keep your secrets."

She gasped.

I laughed.

"Oh, you naughty girl. You tease me."

"So where is Jasper, anyway?" I asked as we got out of the car and headed toward the building.

"Papa show him the ropes. He want new son to run Aphrodite's one day." She eyed me closely. "Unless *you* want to run the restaurant."

"Oh, no. The green-eyed monster is gone. My dear

brother is welcome to the restaurant. That takes the pressure off me."

She grunted. "Ay, so you can make scandalous clothes."

"Which I'm pretty sure every member of our extended family has worn." I opened the door and let her go in first.

*Saved by Roman Cromwell*, I thought, thanking Zeus.

Roman was a middle-aged bald man who was in great shape. He had a black goatee and expensive tastes. His suit was designer, his shoes shined to perfection, and his watch looked like it cost more than my car.

"Ladies, could I offer you anything to drink?" He gestured to a sidebar that had everything from coffee, tea, water and soda to top shelf liquor and wine.

"Oh, my." Ma looked at him all starry-eyed as she patted her beehive. "I have wine spritzer. It five o-clock over there."

Roman looked across the room with a puckered brow. Shrugged, then walked over to make the drink.

"Over where?" I whispered.

"I no where. *Somewhere*," she whispered back through her teeth. "I no time zones. You no embarrass me."

"Me?"

"What was that?" Roman asked as he handed the fizzy drink to ma.

"Nothing for me," I said.

"Ah, well, if you change your mind, just let me know."

One of us had to keep a clear head. Roman was smooth. He probably got all his clients tipsy and then they ended up adding way more than they had planned to a party. That wasn't about to happen on my watch.

"Thanks, but I have to go back to work soon."

"Then, by all means, let's get started." He led the way into the conference room.

We all took our seats at a long, oval table. Roman spread all sorts of pamphlets in front of us, and Ma's eyes lit up. It was either over the endless possibilities or the fizzy drink going straight to her head.

I noticed Mr. Smooth Operator didn't offer any food.

"Are there prices to go with all these ideas?" I asked.

"Funny you should ask." Cameron Oswald walked in with just a walking boot—no more crutches—and sat down across from us by Roman with a folder in her hand.

"Cameron, hi. I didn't know you were Roman's assistant," I said.

"I'm not." Cameron sat up straighter.

"She's my new partner," Roman responded, and so many question entered my mind. The biggest being...

How long have Roman and Cameron been planning on being partners, and did they conspire to kill Delilah to get her out of the way?

## 16

"I can't believe it." Jaz stared, still in a daze as Boomer and her walked over to the table in Nik's kitchen. "The vet confirmed that the twins were both in heat. That is the last thing I wanted to hear."

"Oh, boy." I winced. "Wine?"

"Definitely."

I poured us each a glass while Nik popped open a beer for Boomer and himself. He handed the beer to Boomer and sat down.

"Thanks, man." Boomer took a long gulp, running a hand through his russet hair, then joining him at the table.

Jaz sipped her wine, then shook her head and let out a big sigh. "We won't be able to do a sonogram for a few weeks to confirm if either of them is pregnant, but the vet said Wolfgang is quite the stud."

Wolf let out a woof, earning him scowls from everyone.

He whined and walked out of the room.

"Anyway, the odds are Chanel and Versace are both going to have fur babies around two months from now. That means a whole lot of Saint Berdoodles." Jaz crossed her arms and tapped her foot. "What do you have to say about your boy?"

Nik looked at Boomer and raised an eyebrow.

Boomer shrugged, lifting his hand in the air, palm up, then took another drink.

"He's an animal," Nik said, dryly.

"He sure is." Jaz pointed a finger at Nik. "You should have talked to him about protection and the consequences of what happens when it's not used."

"I repeat...he's an animal." Nik arched a thick black brow.

"A Berdoodle litter can range from six to ten puppies. Times that by two, Detective." Jaz stared him down. "What do you plan to do with your half?"

"*My* half?" Nik gaped.

"Your *boy* knocked my girls up."

"Your *girls* trespassed into my yard."

"Hey, man, we both already have dogs, and Jaz and I have a wedding to plan. It's only fair we split custody," Boomer said. "This isn't 101 Berdoodles."

"Exactly." Jaz pursed her lips.

"Guys," I held up my hand, palm forward, in a wait position, "let's table this conversation until we know for sure if there are even any litters to split. Okay?" I looked them each in the eyes. "We still have a couple of murders to solve."

"We?" both Boomer and Nik said.

"Don't you think it's time we move past that?" I said. "Viggo is family. Four pairs of eyes and ears can't hurt."

"Fine," Nik said in full Detective Stevens mode now and pulled out the small notebook he always kept on him when he was in the middle of a case. "I tracked Zelda down at the Clearview Motel and asked her about the stranger who threatened Viggo."

"What did she have to say?" Boomer looked up from his own notes.

"She said she didn't know who I was talking about, so I described him to her. Distinguished, middle aged, gray hair slicked back in a short ponytail. She said she'd seen him around town but had no idea who he was."

"Then Viggo was lying," I said. "He doesn't work at the modeling agency."

"The name of the agency is Horizon's Modeling Agency." Boomer flipped through his notes. "The CEO confirmed he'd never heard of the guy I described. But he also said Viggo has contractual obligations to them, and they intend to sue him if he doesn't meet his obligations. I told them he can't do anything until the murder investigation is finished. They basically ignored that part and said to let him know they plan to uphold the contract at any cost."

"That seems a little heavy handed if you ask me," Jaz said.

"I'm sure he cost them a lot of money by bailing on that last shoot," Nik pointed out. "Viggo is a lot of things, but he's never been a quitter. There had to be a reason he left. However, a contract is a contract. He's gonna need a good lawyer."

"He's going to need one anyway if we can't clear his name," I added.

"Thalia knows a good one from the city." Nik made a note.

"What about Knox?" I asked. "I saw him in Flannigan's Pub talking to the stranger. He must know him."

"I tracked Knox down and found him at the carnival, arguing with Dixie. She stormed off before I could reach them, but I caught up with him," Nik said. "He said that he *didn't* know John Smith. I looked it up. Of course, the guy used an alias. Knox said he'd just met the man. That the guy asked if Zelda and Viggo were a couple, and Knox told them no. That they dated once, but she was obsessed with him ever since. Viggo didn't even like her much, so there had to be a reason he was hanging out with her. The guy offered Knox money to find out what was going on between them. Knox tried, but Zelda wasn't talking."

"Yeah, I wondered why he was hanging out with her, after he made it clear when he first arrived that he wasn't into her." I raised a brow.

"Maybe he changed his mind after Delilah was murdered and then he got hurt," Jaz said. "And then Mack was murdered. Murder can make a person reflect on their life and give old flames a second chance." She looked at Boomer. "Right, darling?"

"We would have ended up together even if you hadn't been accused of murder," Boomer said. "It was all part of my master plan." He rubbed his hands together.

"Oh, really now? If I recall, you made me pretty angry back in those days with your stubborn, arrogant ways." Jaz poked a finger in his chest. "You would have had to do something pretty bold to get my attention."

"Like what? Throw myself off a roof?"

"That wasn't bold. That was flat out stupid," Nik said dryly.

"Did Viggo ever say why he did that?"

"He claims he was practicing a move he once used in a commercial."

"And you believe him?" I asked.

"Not a chance."

~

THE NEXT MORNING, Ma called me while I was in my loft working on my Kalli Originals spring line. I pinned another piece of lace to my mannequin before answering. I didn't want to lose my train of thought for this outfit and talking to my ma tended to make me lose my mind, period.

"Hi, Ma, what's going on?" I set down my pins.

"It's Aunt Tasoula," Ma said, her tone sounding grave.

My heart sped up. "What's wrong with her?"

Ma grunted. "What *not* wrong with her?"

I calmed down a little. "Okay, let me rephrase that? What's wrong with her *this* time?" My ma and my aunt were so dramatic, it was impossible to tell if something was an emergency or not.

"She have horrible toothache in the night."

"Oh, no. That's awful." I hated going to the doctor, but I especially hated visiting the dentist. Just the thought of someone's hands in my mouth made me gag. It didn't matter that the instruments were sterilized and the hands were covered with plastic gloves.

"Tate call Doc Merigold. Poor man got out of bed and open up just for her. She so demanding."

"Ma, a toothache can be very painful." Doc Merigold was an oral surgeon, and we were lucky to have him right in town.

"Good he open for her. Not good she have wisdom teeth out."

"Well, they say we really don't use or need our wisdom teeth, so if it stops her pain, then it will be worth it."

"Good. It's settled."

I blinked. "What's settled, Ma?"

"You no listen, Kalliope." Ma sighed as if I were the one giving *her* a headache. "You come with me."

"I am listening, but you're not making any sense." I rubbed my temples. "Where exactly are we going?"

"To pick up your aunt. I no deal with her crazy alone."

I frowned. "But I thought Tate was with her?"

"He have to work." Ma grunted. "I have to work too, but your pop say I gotta go. She's my sister. I say she gonna owe me for this."

"Okay, Ma. I'll pick you up."

"I no ride that matchbox car of yours. I drive. Be out front." She hung up.

Just another day in the Twilight Zone with my family.

Ten minutes later, Ma and I were pulling into the parking lot of Doc Merigold's office. We walked inside to find the doctor and a nurse, trying to keep Aunt Tasoula in her chair. She was swinging her legs and singing, *Twinkle, Twinkle, Little Star.*

"Tasoula, you need to bite down and stop singing." Nurse Betty Walker wore tooth fairy scrubs and an understanding albeit tired smile as she tried to hold my aunt still.

"I see stars." Aunt Tasoula wore purple flannel pajamas and big, fuzzy slippers. Purple was her favorite color. "They sooo bright."

"If you don't stop singing and talking, the bleeding won't stop." Doc Merigold put fresh gauze in her mouth. "Now bite down again for me."

"I bleeding?" Aunt Tasoula said around a mouthful of cotton as she kept poking her chin with her finger and giggling. "Why I bleeding?"

"You came to me with a toothache. Your wisdom teeth were so bad, I had to remove them through emergency surgery." He checked her pupils and looked at us. "She'll be a little loopy for a while." He handed Ma a prescription. "Stay ahead of the pain with over-the-counter pain medicine. If her pain gets too bad after the numbness wears off, you can give her one of these instead."

"What do I take when *my* pain get bad?" Ma grunted and took the script.

"Your pain?" Doc asked, looking confused.

"She's kidding," I said, stepping in front of Ma. "She'll be fine. When can we take my aunt home?"

"She's all yours." Doc looked tired in his wrinkled, blood-stained lab coat with his gray hair a mess and glasses askew. "I cancelled my appointments this morning. I'm going home to get some sleep."

"Thank you, Doc," I said. "We all appreciate you coming to Aunt Tasoula's aid in the middle of the night."

"My pleasure. No one deserves to be in pain." He left the room and the nurse got Aunt Tasoula's things ready.

Ma walked over to her sister who was still poking her face and staring at her hand in fascination. "Soula, we here to take you home," Ma shouted. "Can you hear me? Read my lips. Blink twice if you okay."

Aunt Tasoula started blinking rapidly, her eyelashes looking like windshield wipers in a thunderstorm.

"Aunt Tasoula, you can stop blinking."

"Good, I dizzy."

"I bet." I turned to my ma. "Why are you shouting? She had her teeth out, not her eardrums or her vocal chords."

"Then why she blink?" Ma pointed at my aunt.

"Because you told her to, and she's not exactly of the right mind at the moment, if you know what I mean."

Aunt Tasoula gasped. "I have the wrong mind?" She shouted toward the door. "Doc, put my mind back. You gave me someone else's, and I no like it."

"You are nuts." Ma chuckled, looking at her sister.

"No, Monk the Chip is storing nuts in my cheeks. See?" My aunt patted her face. "I no find them." She patted her face again. "I no feel my cheeks." Her eyes widened. "Are they gone too?"

"Oh, no, they're not gone." I stared at her face that was growing rounder and bigger by the moment. "They're definitely right where you left them...and then some."

"Good." She grinned. "I like my cheeks."

"I like your cheeks, too, Aunt Tasoula." I couldn't help smiling in return.

"You both nuts." Ma walked around to stand on one side of my aunt, and I stood on the other.

"Let's go, 'Soula. Time to get you looney tune behind back home." Ma bent over her and slid her hand under her back to help her up.

Aunt Tasoula plunged her own hand in Ma's beehive of hair and started poking around. "Come out, come out wherever you are."

"What you doing?" Ma screeched. "Stop that." She slapped at her hand. "You messing up my hive."

"I look for my wisdom." My aunt pulled on her hand, but it didn't budge.

"Aunt Tasoula, they took your wisdom teeth out," I said, working to free her hand from Ma's hair before she did permanent damage.

"No, it's the goblins. That lame Kopsomesitis *stole* my wisdom. I eat pancakes with honey late last night, and he has weakness for that. He gave me toothache and stole my wisdom," she wailed. "Woe is me, what am I to do with no wisdom."

Finally, I freed my aunt's hand and helped her to her feet. "Maybe we can find it at home, okay? Let's go for a ride." Loopy wasn't a strong enough word to describe my aunt at the moment. It was going to be a long day.

"You no find it at home." Ma rubbed her head while wincing and scowling simultaneously. She thrust her finger in her sister's face. "You can't steal wisdom if you never had it."

Correction...it was going to be a very long week.

"Do you think we have enough supplies?" I asked Jaz.

"I think we're donating more than enough," Jaz replied.

We each carried a bag of hats, scarfs, mittens, and buttons from Full Disclosure's inventory to Clearview Park's Winter Carnival. The snowman competition was this afternoon in the open field by the gazebo.

Milly Donovan was watching Chanel and Versace for free at her house because she still felt bad about letting them escape, and the Houdinis obviously couldn't be trusted alone right now. Jaz didn't want them anywhere near any more male dogs any time soon.

Meanwhile, Wolfgang lost his fresh air privileges without supervision for the foreseeable future aka no cracked sliding glass door while Nik was gone. Nik and Boomer were chasing down more leads with Captain Crenshaw breathing down their necks. Mayor Zimmerman and Senator West were more of a hindrance than a help as they fought for their own agendas instead of working together in trying to help the town.

Basically, everything was a mess.

"How's your aunt doing?" Jaz asked.

It had been a couple of days since Aunt Tasoula had her wisdom teeth out.

"She's driving everyone crazy, especially Ma, who was in charge of taking care of her. Aunt Tasoula is very social. Being housebound is making her go mad. She's being difficult at best and mischievous the rest of the time."

"Oh, boy. Your poor Ma."

"Ma's not handling it well, either, but YiaYia is busy taking care of Frona. There really isn't anyone else." I spotted the gazebo and headed for it as I talked. "Aunt Tasoula wanted out of the house to look for her wisdom, but Ma wouldn't let her. Ma called her a nincompoop and told her to stay put. It was too soon to go out. Aunt Tasoula said the monks were still chipping in her cheeks, trying to steal her mind like they did her wisdom."

"You're giving me a headache just trying to follow that." Jaz winced. "Did they give your aunt pain medication? Because she sounds a little loopy still."

"My aunt's always loopy. She said she lost her pain medication on the first day home." I shook my head. "That doesn't really surprise me. Apparently, she prefers Ouzo to dull the pain anyway."

"Yikes." Jaz raised her brows. "We all know what she gets like when she's had too much Ouzo. Remember the strip club?"

"How could I forget." I shuddered.

"What about her salon?"

"The family is all pitching in to run her Hera's Halo while she recovers. It's what we do." I shrugged. "She has other hair stylists who work for her, but family is family."

"I know they can drive you crazy, but you're so lucky to have a big family. I only have my mother and father. Mom's always gone on modeling gigs, and Dad's a bigwig banker in the city. I don't see them much. I guess that's why I want a big family of my own."

"Does Boomer?" I wondered if she'd had the talk with him, and how she approached it. I was about to ask her when she responded.

"He's warming up to the idea." Jaz winked.

"What did—"

"Speaking of families, look. There's Viggo." Jaz pointed past the snowman contest to the ice rink, and the moment was lost.

"Yeah, and he's with Zelda again. They look like they're arguing. I don't get it. He claims he's not interested in her, yet we keep seeing them together. And when they are together, he looks miserable. So why stay?"

"That is a very good question." Jaz dropped her bag in the donation spot in the judge's gazebo, and I followed suit.

"Oh, thank you so much, ladies." Lois Flannigan was volunteering to judge the snowman competition. She handed Jaz a receipt. "Theresa and Yvonne will be here any moment. Are you staying to watch?"

"Wish we could, but we have to get back to our own booth." Jaz tucked the receipt into her purse.

"Thanks, Lois." I waved as we started to walk away. "Say hi to the ladies and tell them sorry we missed them."

"Will do." She beamed and waved back, watching us go.

"This isn't the way back to our booth." I looked at Jaz curiously.

"Nope, I thought we could check out the speed skating competition." A devilish grin crossed her face. "I've always found those one-piece unitards fascinating. The shiny, bright material covers their entire body. With their hands in streamlined gloves and small goggles over their eyes, their cheeks are the only things showing. Very aerodynamic and eye catching from a fashion point of view."

"And the fact that Viggo and Zelda are over there has nothing to do with your sudden interest?" I raised a brow.

"If we happen to run into them while watching the event, then our detectives can't accuse us of butting into their investigation, now, can they?"

"And this is why I love you." I grinned.

"That's what sidekicks are for." She rubbed her hands together. "Let's go."

We walked by Mayor Zimmerman, being interviewed by the local news crew about the Winter Carnival and updating the press on the murder investigations. Senator West was with Thalia, and they were talking to Yanni and Claudett in the bleachers in front of the ice rink. Meanwhile, Zelda and Viggo were arguing off to the side as we approached.

I glanced at the speed skaters skating in slow laps around the rink, warming up for the main event. It was hard to tell who anyone was in those uniforms, and that was the point. The Masked Skater was the main attraction. They were all local people and half the fun was in guessing who was competing in this year's event.

Jaz walked right up to Viggo, not wasting any time. "Viggo, nice to see you again." Her eyes widened dramatically, and her hand fluttered over her chest. "Oh, I'm so sorry. Am I interrupting anything?"

Viggo's face was flushed. He shook back his thick blond locks of hair and relaxed his massive shoulders as his full lips tipped up in a half smile he knew made most women weak in the knees. "Not at all. Your timing is perfect, Jazlyn." Her name rolled off his tongue as his sizzling blue gaze settled on her.

This time Jaz was the one to blush.

"Really?" I asked, immune to his effects and lacing my words with concern. "Because it looked like you two were arguing."

Zelda's lips were pursed into a pout as she tightened her mink coat. "We had a simple lovers' quarrel. It happens to every couple at times. Right, darling?" She stared at Viggo with icy lavender eyes.

He pulled his gaze away from Jaz and lost his smile as he replied, "Sure."

I touched Zelda's arm. *Don't push me, Viggo. You're not in a position to call the shots.* She suddenly noticed I was touching her arm. "Excuse me." She looked down her perfect aristocratic nose at me.

I let go. "I was just seeing how soft your coat was." Thankfully, my gift worked through clothing.

She relaxed and flipped her thick, long, luscious hair over her shoulder. "Yes, isn't it magnificent?"

"It sure is something."

Her smile slipped. She turned her back on me. "I'm bored, Viggo. Can we leave now? I want to go back to the hotel."

"Whatever you want, *darling*. I wouldn't dream of disappointing you." He gave one last weary, parting glance at Jaz and me. "Ladies." Then tipped his head and walked away with Zelda hanging onto his arm and every woman at the carnival looking on with jealousy.

"That was weird." Jaz watched them disappear around the corner.

"Even weirder was her thinking, *Don't push me, Viggo. You're not in a position to call the shots.*"

"I saw that. Nice move, by the way." Jaz nodded with a grin, then puckered her brow. "What do you think she meant by that thought?"

"That she was in charge." I stared after the direction they had gone, realizing he had shaken off her arm as soon as they were far enough away from anyone watching, but I had seen. "In charge of what is the question."

We heard the Zamboni fire up, ready to clear the ice. That meant the race was about to start. Suddenly, Ma appeared out of nowhere and came running up to us.

"Have you seen that crazy woman?" Ma looked around us frantically, walking in circles with her hand shielding her eyes.

"Who, Aunt Tasoula?" I asked.

"Who else?" Ma paused in her laps to throw up her hands. "I turn my back for one minute, and she escape. That one is sneakier than the goblins."

"Why would you think she's here?" Jaz asked.

"Because I look everywhere else in town. She no anywhere else."

"Well, we haven't seen her." I studied my ma with concern. "Why are you so worried?"

Ma stopped walking and looked me in the eyes. "She bring along her little friend...Mr. Ouzo."

"Oh, boy." I cringed.

"Oh, no." Jaz winced.

"It's Barney the dinosaur," someone yelled.

"It's a Power Ranger," someone else shouted.

"It's one of the Wiggles," a third person chimed in.

We all looked over towards the ice rink, and children were cheering as if the mayor had hired a character costume skater as entertainment before the speed skate competition. A big purple blob consisting of fuzzy onesie pajamas with the hood up, a fuzzy scarf, thick fuzzy mittens, and big ski goggles zigzagged wobbling across the ice on massive hockey skates that looked suspiciously like Pop's, while pushing a broom.

"That sure doesn't look like Leonard," Jaz said.

Leonard the maintenance man was the one who had volunteered to create and maintain the ice for the weeklong carnival.

Suddenly, the Fred Astaire Ice Capades wannabe shouted, "Opa!" and drained the last of a bottle of Ouzo.

"Tasoula!" Ma shouted.

The purple head turned our way and gaped at us through lopsided goggles. All we saw were big, magnified eyes and massive chipmunk cheeks.

"Ophelia?" Aunt Tasoula waved.

"Look out!" I pointed as the Zamboni was headed directly for her.

Tate hopped onto a nearby emergency snowmobile and raced onto the ice in record time, sweeping her off her feet.

"Adonis, take me away," Aunt Tasoula yelled.

The Zamboni swerved to miss them and crashed into the side of the ice rink, while Tate's snowmobile skidded to a stop with Aunt Tasoula flying over Tate's head and landing in the snowbank. Everyone went running over to help, and Leonard lead the way with his toolkit in hand and an angry look on his face.

"Tasoula, what were you thinking?" Ma asked, out of breath as we reached my aunt's side.

"I *no* think, Ophelia," Aunt Tasoula wailed. "I have no wisdom left. It's terribly sad. I just want to speed skate, but Amos skates too big. And smelly." She waved her mitten in front of her nose, then she grinned. "I give me eight out of ten for dismount, though." She got up and bowed.

"And I'm out of patience." Ma pointed her finger at her sister. "Amos no gonna like this. One more thing he gonna have to pay to fix. That mean you gonna owe me, and then you find out what being sad really feels like."

THAT EVENING I brought takeout over to Chloe's house.

"Nik said you weren't feeling well." I carried Ma's homemade chicken noodle soup and crusty Greek bread with crackers over to her kitchen table.

"Awe, thank you, honey. I just have a head cold. I told Quincy to stay away from me. He can't afford to get sick with these murder investigations still going on." She wore flannel pajamas and a thick fuzzy robe and slippers. Her nose was red, and she carried a box of tissues around with her.

"I don't blame you. It's that time of year for colds and the flu. Do you have Vitamin C and Zinc?" I squirted hand sanitizer into my hands and rubbed thoroughly, careful not to touch anything as I stayed six feet away from her.

"My Nikos brought me some earlier today. He's such a good boy." Her face softened with love and pride.

"He sure is. I'm very lucky."

"I would say he's pretty lucky, too." She sat down at the table, propped her sore knee on a chair, and opened the bag of food. "This looks delicious." She took a spoonful and slurped it with a sigh.

I sat down at the table across from her. "I'm so glad you like it."

"Thank your mama for me, and you, too." She studied me with fondness and appreciation in her dark eyes. "That was very sweet of you."

"You're very welcome." I paused a moment to settle my racing heart. "Can I ask you a question."

"Of course."

I searched for the right words, and then just decided to go for it. "Do you know if Nik wants children?"

Her eyes sprang wide. "Oh, my. I no expect that. Is there something you want to tell me?" Her gaze dropped to my stomach.

"Oh, my Zeus, no." I laughed a little hysterically.

She gave me a funny look. "Then why you ask?"

I inhaled a big breath. "I'm not pregnant, and no, your son has not asked me to marry him. He did ask to knock down the wall between our apartments and move in together. Jaz has already agreed to sell us the house if we do that."

Chloe took a minute to eat some soup. "That's a big step."

"I know." I played with a napkin in front of me on the table, ripping off little pieces. "I'm still thinking on it."

She nodded. "It's good to think on things."

"That also got me thinking about life in general. I started wondering if I even wanted children, which I'm not sure I could handle all that goes along with that." Birthing babies, dirty diapers, spit up. I shuddered just thinking about the germs.

"That's true. Babies aren't easy."

"That's for sure." I nodded. "And then I realized I have never asked Nik if he wants children. I thought maybe you might know. I mean, he was engaged before, which I also just found out about."

"He never talks about babies, but that doesn't mean he no want any. I hope he wants some. He's my only child. I can't imagine not being a grandmama. But he can't do this for me. He has to want them for himself. You, too." She patted my hand. *I think this a conversation you need to have with my Nikos.* She let go of my hand and went back to eating her soup.

"I know, you're right. I do need to talk to Nik about this."

She blinked. "Did I say that out loud?"

*Whoops.* "Uh..."

Nik came bursting through the door with Viggo, just in time. I breathed a sigh of relief, until I saw his face.

"This cold must have gone straight to my head." Chloe looked up and saw Nik, too. "Nikos, what's wrong?"

"Your nephew, that's what's wrong." Nik stood there with his hands on his hips, glaring at his cousin.

"Viggo, what you do now?" Chloe sighed.

"He tried to refill a prescription for more pain meds, but the pharmacy called Doc LaLone." Nik stared at Viggo with a mixture of confusion and frustration. "Doc said no, he didn't authorize them to be refilled. Why would you forge a prescription?"

"Because I'm in pain. I went to Doc LaLone first. He said I didn't need more pain medicine. That I should be enough better to just use over-the-counter medication, but he's not me." Viggo tapped his ribs and held up his arm. "I'm still in pain. He doesn't know what that feels like."

"If he thought you should have more, he would have prescribed them," Nik ground out and shook his head. "I am trying to keep you out of jail for your parents' sake, but you are making it nearly impossible. You're lucky Doc didn't turn you in. He covered for you with the pharmacy and said it was a mistake on his part."

"Well, I would give you mine, but I must have thrown them out." Chloe blew her nose. "I'm sorry you're in pain."

"Does this have anything to do with Zelda?" I asked, and all eyes turned toward me. "Because it's clear she's holding something over your head."

Viggo's eyes widened, but then he masked his expression. He didn't say a word, he just went to his room.

Nik looked at me. "Looks like someone just hit a nerve." He nodded. "You're on to something, Ballas. This question is, what exactly does Zelda know that we don't?"

**18**

I was walking up and down the aisles of our local grocery store, buying food for a nice dinner with Nik. I knew I needed to have that talk about what both of our goals looked like for the future. What was the point of moving in together, or even falling more in love with each other, if our goals didn't align.

The thought of breaking up devastated me, but I couldn't imagine what it would be like if we waited to have this conversation down the road. I already loved him so much and couldn't imagine my life without him. I just didn't know what that life looked like.

Sal's Supermarket was now called Stallones. Since Salvatore had passed away, his widow took over the family business and changed it to their last name. She was having a hard time coping with him gone.

Nik wasn't dying, but our relationship might be.

I couldn't even think about that right now. So, I focused on what I was going to make for dinner. Maybe I would make spicy chicken kabobs with lemon potatoes. Nik loved that, and it wasn't too difficult.

I picked up a pack of chicken, yellow peppers, cherry tomatoes, and potatoes. Heading to the spice aisle for cumin, cilantro, and chili paste, I heard hushed voices. It wasn't busy today, so there weren't that many people in the store.

Creeping closer, I peeked around an endcap.

Knox Young smoothed a hand over his slicked-back black hair. He wore designer jeans and a sweater with fancy shoes and a short wool coat. He stood beside a half-full shopping cart, talking to John Smith aka the silver fox.

John wore his hair in his usual low man bun, his face chiseled and full of class and something else. He stood there in his expensive suit, calmly waiting with his hands folded in front of him, yet there was an edge of danger that lurked just beneath the surface.

"Look, man, I don't have any answers for you yet." Knox shoved his hands in his jeans' pockets.

"Do you want to get paid the rest of the money?"

"Yes, of course. I need the money until my next gig. I've never been good at budgeting my paychecks to last me between gigs. After Viggo screwed everything up, I don't even know when my next gig will be."

"I already gave you a down payment. If you can't get me the information I want in a timely manner, then I expect to get paid back with interest."

"I-I'm not going to be able to pay you back the down payment," Knox sputtered. "I already spent that money. You're going to have to be patient. Why do you want to know so much about Viggo and Zelda, anyway?"

"What my employer does with that information is none of your business, and I'm about out of patience." His eyes grew deadly. "If you can't pay the money back, we will take out the funds in other ways."

"What does that mean?" Knox squeaked. It was

clear he wasn't used to dealing with people of this nature.

"Trust me." John cracked his knuckles. "You don't want to find out."

"Okay, okay." Knox held his hands up in front of him. "Look, I'm wearing Zelda down. She's getting pretty sick of Viggo's hot and cold treatment toward her. I'm sure I can get her to talk about what she's blackmailing him for soon."

"See that you do." John started walking my way.

I slipped back into my aisle and began adding seasonings to my cart. Suddenly, I felt eyes on me like daggers stabbing me in the back.

"What are you thinking, Ms. Ballas?" said a smooth, rich, male voice.

I whipped around and looked up. John Smith stood not more than one foot away from me. I didn't know how he knew my name, but two could play at that game.

I tried to still my racing heart. "Whatever do you mean, Mr. Smith?"

A muscle in his cheek twitched. "What are you thinking of making with all that?" He gestured to the food in my cart. "I'm new in town, but I've heard enough to know your parents' restaurant is one of the best. I like to cook." He tipped his head and folded his hands in front of him again. "You know, stir the pot."

"Well, this dish isn't made in a pot. It's made on the grill." I tipped my head and folded my hands, resting them on my shopping car. "You know, slowly roast your prey until it gives you exactly what you want."

His gaze narrowed ever so slightly. He knew I'd overheard him with Knox. I didn't know if that was good or bad.

"It sounds perfect," he said carefully. "You'd better

be careful you don't turn the heat up too much." His eyes locked onto mine, and a chill slithered down my spine. "I wouldn't want you to get burned."

"Oh, don't you worry about me being in danger." I stared right back, refusing to flinch or cower. "I know a thing or two about protecting myself."

"Safety first." He saluted me with two fingers and started walking away, saying over his shoulder, "You have a good day now."

I did *not* wish him the same.

I headed straight for the self-checkout line, purchased my items, then made my way to the parking lot. I stored my groceries in the trunk and was about to slide into the driver's seat when I noticed my aunt sitting in the passenger side of Ma's car.

I hadn't realized my ma was here.

I closed my door and started walking over to talk to my aunt, but then stopped in my tracks. John Smith came out of the store, not carrying a single bag with him. To my shock, he opened the door to Ma's car and climbed into the driver's side.

I heard my aunt gasp. "Well, you're not my sister," she finally managed.

She had the window cracked.

"No, I am not," he said. "Seems to me you're a little lost."

I hurried my steps to reach them, but I was too late.

He started the engine and gunned it. "Where you headed. I'll drop you off," I heard before he locked the doors and pulled away, looking straight at me in the rear-view-mirror with a knowing smile.

Did he just steal Ma's car?

I pulled out my phone, ready to call Nik.

"Kalli?" Ma asked. "What you doing here?"

"Grocery shopping. I was about to call Nik. Ma, I don't know how to tell you this, but someone just stole your car."

"What?" She ran past me and hit her key fob.

A horn beeped.

She looked at me like I was nuts and pointed to the parking lot. "They no steal my car. It's right there. Did you lose you wisdom, too?"

"Apparently so," I muttered and looked toward the parking lot.

Sure enough, there was Ma's car. John Smith must have rented a car exactly like that. Why? To mess with my family? Or frame one of us for something? My mind was racing with possibilities.

"Now where did that crazy woman go?"

"You mean Aunt Tasoula?" I'd almost forgotten my aunt was riding around with a maniac at this very moment.

"I tell her to stay in the car, but she come in anyway. So, I send her back out. Why she no do what I tell her?"

"Oh, she did as you told her to, all right."

"How?" Ma pointed to her empty car.

"She got in the wrong car."

"What?" Ma put her hands on her beehive. "She gonna be the death of me yet."

"You and me both. There is still one—possibly two —killers out there."

Ma's face paled. "Well, where is she now?"

"Off to Lord only knows where with a man I don't trust."

THE NEXT DAY was the last day of the Winter Carnival. Aunt Tasoula was at home when Mom and I got there. Said some really nice gentleman dropped her off after she got in his rental car by mistake. He was definitely messing with me, and now he knew where my family lived. His message was clear...

Back off or else he would mess with my family for real.

Needless to say, my special dinner never happened. But today was a new day. A clean slate. A day to start fresh. My whole family, as well as Nik's, was at the Winter Carnival. A big parade was planned. The weather was iffy with big fat flakes falling, but the show must go on, as they say.

Leonard made sure the snowplows were in tip top shape and ready to go. The snowplow drivers had plowed and sanded the roads, and the floats were all lined up and ready by the park. People filled the streets, claiming their spots along the curbs as they waited for the big event to roll past them.

"Kalli, there you are." Sherry and Yvonne joined me on the sidewalk. "We just bought our valentine's lingerie from your new line. I had no idea you had modest full-length pajamas for mature women."

"Speak for yourself," Yvonne added with a sly smile. "I haven't aged that much, and I'm certainly not modest."

"Well, when you do, you'll appreciate the elegant additions included in Kalli's line. I feel so beautiful yet sexy."

"That's because you *are* beautiful and sexy." I smiled, meaning it.

I loved being inclusive for women of all ages and sizes, wanting them to know I saw them and heard their requests for lingerie that fit any woman with as much or as little coverage as they wanted, making her feel sexy yet comfortable in her own body. So, I had expanded my line to be inclusive.

"Well, hopefully our husbands think so, too." Sherry blushed. "I plan to surprise Bennett on Valentine's Day."

"Well, I for one, bought my lingerie for me." Yvonne smoothed back her chic hair. "Because I'm worth it."

"Good for you," I said. "Speaking of your husbands, where are they?"

"Probably getting more food." Sherry laughed.

"And shopping. They haven't found exactly what they're looking for, but that's okay. Sherry and I have been benefitting nicely." Yvonne flashed a watch and pointed to a pair of earrings she sported, then winked at Sherry.

"They're supposed to meet us for the parade, though." Sherry looked at her watch. "I hope they hurry or they're going to miss it."

"Hopefully the weather turns around. Enjoy the parade, ladies." I pulled my hat down over my ears. "I have to go find my family." I waved to them and traveled down the street.

I saw Nik, Boomer, and Jaz. Boomer and Jaz were a little further down by my parents, claiming their spot on the curb, while Nik walked off to meet me halfway.

"There you are," I said as Nik came to a stop by my side.

"Here I am." Nik kissed my cheek. *You okay? You've been acting different lately. Is something wrong?*

"I'm fine, I promise." I smiled at him. "I just have a lot on my mind."

"I hear that." He blew out a breath. "I'm getting really worried Viggo is going to end up in jail."

"I don't think he will." I glanced around, looking for John Smith or Knox. "There are too many other suspicious people in town."

"Yeah, but Viggo's not innocent, either. He's hiding something. I don't know what we're missing."

"I know what we're missing." I looked over to see Ma, Pop, and Tate. "Where's Aunt Tasoula?" Ever since John Smith drove her home, she made me nervous. If he ended up hurting any of my family, I would be devastated.

"Let's go see." Nik took my hand, kissed the back of it, and then ledme the rest of the way over to my family.

The parade wouldn't start for another fifteen minutes. Tate was supposed to lead the procession by driving the town's truck that would pull the main float with Mayor Zimmerman on it. Aunt Tasoula had stopped drinking the Ouzo. Her swelling had gone down, and she no longer needed Ma to babysit her.

"Hi guys, are you ready for the parade?" I rubbed my hands together, trying to get warm. "Aren't you leading the parade?" I asked Tate.

"Yes, in fact, I should head over there now. I just got a call. The town's truck broke down, so I told Leonard to hook up my truck to the float. I left it unlocked with the keys inside." He held up his hand at Nik and Boomer's look. "I know, not smart, but who's gonna mess with me?"

He had a point. He might be older, but he was nearly as big as Nik and Viggo.

Tate looked at his watch. "Your aunt should have been back by now. Tell her I'll see her at the end of the parade." He jogged away at a quick pace.

"Where did she go?" Nik asked Ma.

"Oh, now that she is *healed*, she wanna donate a

spa day to the float that wins in the judge's circle." Ma raised her hands, palms up. "She forgot the prize at the salon, so she went to get it. Last minute, of course."

"Aunt Tasoula driving in the snow? That's scary." I looked around but didn't see her. "It concerns me that she's not back yet."

We heard a truck with blaring music coming down the street. We looked down the road, and sure enough, Tate's truck was rolling along at a faster pace than what was expected from someone leading a parade. I looked in the driver's seat, and there sat Aunt Tasoula. She had the radio blasting, looking like a bobblehead as she danced and sang her way down the road, driving way too fast.

Everyone started waving and cheering along the side of the street.

A line of floats slid and weaved along behind the truck, trying to keep up. Good Lord, they must think the parade had started early, so they'd followed my crazy aunt. Did she not know she was pulling a float? Probably not, since the back window was covered with ice, and she'd only cleared the front windshield enough to see.

As it got closer, we saw the mayor hanging onto the float, screaming for help.

Aunt Tasoula saw the people waving, so she started waving back, clueless. She really had lost her wisdom. Forget about giving a prize for the best float. She was about to receive the biggest ticket of her life.

If Ma didn't kill her first.

**19**

"Tell me again what happened?" Captain Crenshaw asked Aunt Tasoula as we sat inside the nearest building from where the parade was held.

Town Hall.

All those involved were sitting in the rows of chairs, waiting their turn. The captain questioned my aunt at a table up front but close enough to hear their conversation. You could have heard a pin drop as all ears were tuned in, trying to make sense of the disaster. The chaos of the Aunt Tasoula Show had ended in multiple vehicles and floats sliding off the road and getting stuck in the snow, but no one got hurt, thank goodness.

"My car got stuck," she held her hands up, "so I borrow Tate's truck. He always leave his keys in it."

"Why were you leaving when the parade was about to start?" The captain took notes as my aunt answered his questions.

She motioned him forward until he leaned down close enough to hear her whisper. "Am I in trouble with you?"

He glanced over his shoulder at one very frazzled,

angry mayor. "It depends on how much trouble I'm in with her."

Aunt Tasoula made the sign of the cross. "Well," she said loud enough for the mayor to hear, "I donate *very* nice prize to winning float." She looked at the captain and shrugged. "I forget prize at my salon." She tapped her temple. "I lose my wisdom, you know."

"So, I've heard." He pinched the bridge of his nose, looking exhausted and disheveled before glancing back at his notes. "Why take Tate's truck instead of calling, oh I don't know, your sister? Niece? Anyone not involved in the parade?"

Aunt Tasoula was already shaking her head. "They all sick of taking care of me." She patted her chest. "I take care of myself."

"Really?" Captain Crenshaw raised a brow. "Because I have yet to see that."

Chloe cleared her throat, giving him a look that said never insult a Greek mama.

He sighed. "Please continue, Tasoula."

"My Tate have very important job, you know." Aunt Tasoula wiggled her fingers at Tate. "I so proud of you."

Tate winked at her and blew her a kiss.

"Anywho, he suppose to lead parade in the town truck." Aunt Tasoula looked at the mayor and raised a brow. "Maybe town money should be spent on fixing *that*."

The mayor's mouth fell open, and she started to speak.

Aunt Tasoula held up her hand. "I no done." She looked back at the captain, ignoring the mayor's grumbles. "I know my Tate no mind if I use his truck. He no using it. I got stuck, remember? My car no good in snow."

"Except Tate *was* using his truck," the captain said.

"But I didn't know that." She held up her hands. "How I supposed to know that?"

"Oh, I don't know, maybe by the large float attached to it?" the captain said carefully, as though talking to a child.

"It snow like avalanche. Tate's truck look like a yeti. My eyes no too good. I no see float attached to it. I clear off front windshield and off I go."

"That's for sure," he grumbled.

"I'm a rock star. Everybody cheer and wave to me." She grinned. "I very popular."

"Not at the moment." He looked her in the eyes with a serious expression. "Did you ever think they might be yelling and waving for you to stop?"

"I no think that." She shook her head sadly. "No wisdom, remember?"

"How could I ever forget?" The captain sighed.

"I no see ice, either. Very scary."

"Yes, it was. When you slid off the road, you caused all the other vehicles to slide off as well. Did you know that?"

"They crazy. They should no have followed me. Very dangerous." She tsked at the other drivers in the audience.

"That's what you do in a parade," Captain Crenshaw said dryly. "Follow the leader."

"Right." She pointed her finger. "So this is their fault."

The captain rubbed his temples as he muttered, "I think you lost more than your wisdom."

"Look, Captain, this is getting us nowhere." Mayor Zimmerman walked over to them with Roman and Cameron flanking her. They'd been doing damage control to save the events after the Ballas shenanigans the entire Winter Carnival. "Someone has to go to jail." The mayor looked at Aunt Tasoula. "This town is counting on me to clean up the streets."

Ma surged to her feet. "You are so right, Mayor Zimmerman. This town," Ma held the mayor's gaze, "made up mostly of Ballas and Pagonis families," she paused another beat, "are most definitely counting on you to do just that." Ma crossed her arms over her chest. "Don't we still have a murderer on the loose? Possibly two?"

The mayor looked around at the people in the chairs, half of whom were family and friends, who were all staring at her with displeasure. Senator West sat next to Thalia with a knowing look in his eyes, and then slipped his arm around her.

"Well, someone at least has to pay for the damages to people's vehicles." The mayor looked at Aunt Tasoula.

"That's fair," Ma said, and then looked at Pop expectantly.

My aunt had taken out a second mortgage on her salon to add the spa and hadn't recouped her expenses yet.

Pop groaned but stood. "Ballas take care of their own. We got it covered." He looked at Ma. "You sisters cost me so much money."

"But we're worth it." Ma pinched his cheek and smiled. "Right?"

Pop hesitated as if giving that honest thought.

Ma's lips formed a flat line. "I say, right?"

"Of course, of course." Pop kissed her cheek.

Ma sat up straight, but her lips softened as she nodded once. "That's better."

"Okay, then," the captain said, "if there's not anything else, I say we're done here. Let's get back to work, gentlemen." He looked at Nik and Boomer as everyone else started filing out of the town hall to head home.

Boomer's cell phone rang. "Detective Matheson here."

Nik and the captain stopped walking.

Boomer frowned. "Calm down, Milly, are the dogs okay?"

Jaz grabbed my hand.

"We'll be right there." He hung up.

"What is it?" Jaz bit her bottom lip.

"The dogs are fine," Boomer reassured her, then looked at the captain. "Milly's husband, not so much."

"What happened?" Nik asked.

"Rockwell Jeweler's has been robbed."

"MILLY, you poor thing. I'm so sorry this happened to Nelson." Jaz held Milly's hand as we sat in her apartment in the back of the jewelry shop.

"Thank you both for coming." Milly wrung her hands together.

"Of course," I said.

"We wouldn't have it any other way," Jaz added.

Boomer and Nik were out in the jewelry store with Nelson and the crime scene investigators, while Jaz and I had come to console Milly and get her side of the story.

"Is Nelson going to be okay?" I gave Chanel and Versace a pet on the tops of their fluffy, black, long-eared poodle heads.

They were clearly picking up on Milly's hysterical mood. They went to lay down on the carpet by the window, curled up together, and finally settled. I sanitized my hands and looked around the room for any clues.

"I took the girls for a walk earlier during the parade. I figured we could all use the exercise. I was going to watch, but the weather got so bad, I figured I'd better not risk it with the baby...both mine and theirs."

"Allegedly." I coughed.

"Most likely." Jaz snorted.

"I'm with Jaz. From one expectant mother to another, I can sense these things." Milly looked over at the dogs who were sleeping soundly now. "Anyway, Nelson decided to stay and do some work in the shop. He was closed for business, working on some jewelry repairs he was commissioned to do in his back workshop, with the door closed."

I searched my mind for what I'd seen when we first got there. "It didn't look like the front door to the jewelry shop was broken into."

"That's the thing," Milly pointed out. "Our cameras are all out front. The thief must have known that and thought we were both gone to the parade. They picked the lock to our apartment in the back and came in through that way. They turned the inside cameras to the jewelry store off through our office then went into the store, not realizing Nelson was still home and in his workshop."

"What happened?" Jaz's eyes grew wide, and her lips parted.

Milly looked off as if searching her memory. "Nelson said he heard a noise, but both the house and the jewelry store were locked. He thought I came back early, so he stepped out of his workshop."

"Did he see anything?" I pulled my little monogramed notebook out of my purse and took some notes.

"No, Nelson said it all happened so fast. The thief must have heard him get up because the person was ready when he came out the door. They jumped him, hit him over the head knocking him out, and then took off."

"That had to be terrifying." Jaz patted Milly's hand.

"It could have been worse. He could have been shot." Milly started crying all over again at that thought. "I'm pretty sure he has a concussion, but he'll live. He refused to go to the hospital until he talked to the police."

I gave her a sympathetic smile. "Do you know if the person who broke in took anything?"

"It doesn't look like it. They didn't touch the jewelry in the display cases. It's like they were looking for things that weren't in plain sight. Like our drawers and cabinets were all rummaged through. And they searched our laptop. Then they left. Very strange for a robbery, don't you think?"

"Very strange indeed." I studied my notes.

Jaz harnessed up her girls and stood. "We won't take up any more of your time, Milly. Let us know how Nelson makes out at the hospital."

"I will. I'll walk your girls out." Milly led us to the front of the shop where Nik and Boomer were waiting with Nelson.

"Max wants to take me by ambulance to the hospital, but he said you can ride along." Nelson held some ice to his head.

"Okay." Milly hugged him.

Max helped them both into the ambulance, then signaled the driver. He waved to us as he climbed in the back to monitor Nelson, shutting the ambulance door seconds before it left with its sirens wailing.

"What is happening to our town?" Jaz tightened her hold on her dog's leashes.

"I thought the break-ins had to do with Dixie Doolittle, but now I'm not so sure." I pulled out my notebook, earning a raised eyebrow from Detective Dreamy. "What? I wrote down my thoughts in case my wisdom got stolen, too." I blinked innocently.

Nik narrowed his eyes. "I'm not buying it, Ballas, but I'll play along. What do you have in that handy, dandy little notebook?"

"The first murder happened at Dixie's house, but it looked like someone was looking for something. I initially thought the break-in had to do with Delilah. Scout said she had followed Delilah there, thinking it was her house. She was looking for something to pawn to make up for the amount Delilah shorted her. But then she saw someone, so she left."

"Correct." Nik waited for me to continue.

"Next, Scout's house gets trashed, again without taking something, like they thought maybe she had found what they were looking for at Dixie's house. They could have followed Delilah and also thought the house was hers."

"True." Nik looked at Boomer.

"But then Dixie's antique shop gets broken into. Her place of business is clearly not linked to Delilah, who was a party planner. Again, they don't take anything. That makes me think the thief is looking for something related to Dixie and not Delilah. Plus, Dixie keeps acting nervous, looking over her shoulder."

Nik checked his own notebook. "Agreed."

"What I don't get is why was someone snooping

around the pawn shop? Leonard said the door was open when he got there the night Mack was murdered, but that Theresa didn't want him to say anything. She said nothing was taken so it was her business. She couldn't afford for her shop to get shut down and become a crime scene. What would the thief want with her if he was after something that Dixie had?"

"Maybe it wasn't a thief." Nik rubbed his jaw and started to pace. I'd come to recognize that was how he pondered possibilities. "Maybe Theresa was having an affair."

"I thought that, too, but then why would the thief break into Nelson's jewelry store and again not take anything?" I tapped my own notebook. "Which now makes me think the break-ins might not be linked to Dixie."

"I didn't have a chance to tell you yet, but Doc said his office was broken into a little while ago. Captain went there since we were here." Boomer looked directly at Nik. "The medicine cabinet was cleared out of controlled medications."

Palpable tension filled the air with what was being left unsaid.

"Ma said she must have misplaced the pain pills Doc gave her for her knee surgery that she never took because she couldn't find them," Nik said gravely.

"My ma had Aunt Tasoula's pain pills for her wisdom teeth surgery, but Aunt Tasoula said she lost them the first day," I added.

"Didn't Viggo just get in trouble for trying to refill his pain pills by forging a script because Doc said no to him?" Jaz asked, earning surprised looks from both Boomer and Nik. "What?" She glanced at me, then back at them. "We tell each other everything. You're just going to have to deal with that."

I wrinkled my nose at Nik and mouthed, *Sorry*.

"I'm beginning to think we know why Viggo jumped off your ma's roof," Boomer said what we all were obviously thinking.

"Pain pill addiction can make people desperate." A muscle in Nik's jaw bulged. "Desperate people do stupid things."

"What are you going to do?" Boomer asked.

"I think it's time my cousin and I had a heart-to-heart."

"What do you mean, he's not here?" Nik asked his ma as we stood in her kitchen. We'd headed straight to her house to look for Viggo while Boomer and Jaz took Chanel and Versace home.

"I come home from town hall, and he no here." Chloe shrugged, sweeping her arms in a circle around her kitchen.

Nik searched the rest of his mother's house, and then returned to the kitchen. "His things are still here, so he didn't skip town."

"Why would he skip town? That make no sense." Chloe crossed her arms over her middle, looking worried.

"He might not have skipped town, but he's been lying to us." Nik looked at the notepad on the kitchen counter and in the mail basket, as if searching for any clues his cousin may have left behind.

"He no lie to me." She shook her head.

"Yes, Ma, he did. I'll explain why later." Nik looked his mother in the eyes. "This is important, Ma, so I need you to concentrate. Can you remember anything else he might have said as to where he planned to go?"

"We think he might be in trouble, Chloe," I said to her. "We just want to help keep him safe."

"I knew this woman gonna get him in trouble." Chloe paced.

"I assume you mean Zelda." Nik narrowed his eyes. "What about her?"

"One minute she with him. The next she with that other guy."

"Knox?" I asked.

"Yes, the one with hair." Chloe nodded. "I worry she two-timing him. I tell Viggo so, but he act like he no care." She shrugged. "He said he was done with her."

"Maybe he was," I speculated.

"Then why I smell her perfume when I get home?"

"Well, Viggo is a big guy," Nik said. "There's no way Zelda could force Viggo to go anywhere, even with a broken arm and cracked ribs."

"Maybe not physically," I pointed out, "but like you said. He's addicted to pain killers, and drug addiction can make people do things we could never imagine."

"Drug addiction?" Chloe gasped. "Oh, woe is me, his mother gonna be so upset."

"Don't worry, Ma." Nik grabbed his keys, looking at me with exasperation over what I had revealed. "I'll find him."

I followed Nik out the door to his car.

"Where do you think you're going?" He turned to me.

I bounced off his chest. "With you."

"Kalli, I don't think—" He held up a hand.

I took his hand in mine. "Then don't think, Nik. We're supposed to be a team. Let me help you, please."

He took a big breath. *What if you get hurt?*

"I won't."

He looked at me. *What if you say something to jeopardize the case?*

"I'll *try* not to."

"Okay. I don't have time to argue about this." He kissed my cheek, then tugged me after him. "Let's go."

We drove to the Clearview Motel.

Larry Miller owned the motel but had since retired and hired a manager. Gary Bolin, who used to be the town drunk and had once had a crush on me, had taken over. Gary and Lisa Chamberlain, who was the bookkeeper for Maria at Sinfully Delicious, were engaged and soon to be married.

Gary sat at the front desk when we walked in. He was a good-looking guy since he'd gotten sober, with sandy blond hair and green eyes. He looked up and smiled when he spotted us. "Hey, guys. How are you?"

"We're doing okay with everything that's going on," I said.

"I heard about your cousin, Detective," Gary said. "If there's anything I can do to help with the investigation, just let me know."

"Actually, have you seen him around here?" Nik asked.

"A time or two." Gary nodded.

"But not today?" I clarified.

"No, sorry."

"What about Zelda Knight or Knox Young?" Nik asked.

Gary checked his ledger. "Looks like they checked out earlier today. A lot of people checked out today now that the Winter Carnival is over. What a week, huh?"

"Don't even get me started," I responded.

"Thanks, Gary." Nik looked at me. "Let's go."

I waved to Gary and hurried after Nik as he

headed out the door with much longer strides than mine. "Where are we going this time?"

"The only other place I can think of. A place tucked out of the way when you want to be secretive about something."

I snapped my fingers. "Lakeshore Heights."

"Bingo. When Viggo first got here and the Clearview Hotel was full, I mentioned this place to him. He didn't want to be away from the action, so he asked if he could stay with me. I reluctantly agreed, but then he went to Ma's place anyway."

We got in the car and headed there in silence.

Lakeshore Heights was just across the town line in Lakeshore. It was a small motel that sat on a little lake tucked into the woods. It was picturesque and modern, with a charming rustic interior. There were animal heads on the wall, but if you could look past that, the wooden accents and scenic paintings gave it a warm cozy feel.

The best part was the cozy cabins down at the Oasis.

We pulled in the driveway and went inside. A man who looked to be in his sixties with chubby cheeks and a round belly gave us a big smile when we approached the front desk. "Well, aren't you two a sweet couple. I have just the room for you. Or would you prefer one of our cozy cabins?" He wagged his eyebrows.

Nik pulled out his badge and looked at the man's nametag. "Neither, Arnold."

"Oh," Arnold stood up straighter, his face flushing red. "I didn't mean to assume you were a couple."

"We are, actually," I clarified.

The man looked back and forth between us then

rubbed his forehead. "So, do you want a room or not, then? I'm confused."

"No." Nik gave me a look, and I didn't need to know how to read his mind to know he was thinking, *you're supposed to be helping. This is not helping. Need to know basis, Ballas. And this guy doesn't need to know we're a couple.* "We're here on official police business, nothing else."

"Why don't you just tell me what you are looking for, and I'll see if I can help. Does that sound good?" Arnold stared up at him.

"Sounds great." Nik looked around. "Do you have anyone staying here by the names of Zelda Knight or Viggo Stevens?"

"Well, I'm really not supposed to divulge that information, but since this is official police business and all, let me take a look." He searched through his computer but then frowned. "I don't see anyone by those names. Sorry."

"What about Knox Young?" Nik tapped the computer.

The man looked again. "Nope, still don't see anyone with that name."

Nik blew out a sigh. "Well, thank you for your help. I appreciate it."

We started to walk away, but then I stopped and turned back. "What about a man named John Smith."

Nik arched a brow at me.

I gave him a look that said, *this is me being helpful.*

The man searched one more time, and then smiled wide. "Yes, here it is. John Smith." He pointed to the screen.

"Which room is he in?" Nik waited expectantly.

"Oh, he didn't want a room. He chose the most secluded cabin down at the lake. I found that odd. That's usually reserved for couples, but he didn't have anyone with him." Arnold shrugged. "Should I ring him that you're on your way."

"No," Nik and I both said at once.

"Oh, my." The man jumped. "Well, okay then."

"Official police business, remember?" Nik's expression was dead serious.

"Thank you again for your help." I smiled with appreciation as we left.

Five minutes later, we were down by the water, hiding outside the cabin, and peeking in through the window.

John Smith was standing on one side of the room next to Knox, while Viggo and Zelda were across the room with the table between them all.

"I told you before, I'm not posing for any more nude photos." Viggo's hands were balled into fists at his sides.

I swallowed a gasp.

Nik's face hardened.

"What are you talking about?" Knox wrinkled his brow. "None of our modeling gigs are nude, man. You're starting to lose it."

"Oh, he's lost it, all right." Zelda crossed her arms and looked at Viggo with disgust. "He's been posing for nude photo shoots in exchange for drugs. The modeling agency *owns* him."

"So *that's* what you were blackmailing him about." Knox looked at her like he didn't even recognize her. "Why? He doesn't want anything to do with you, so why would you want to be with him?"

"No one breaks up with me," she spat. "It looks bad for my image. I don't want him. I just wanted to be the one to publicly break up with him. I threatened to expose him to the world if he didn't go along with my plan."

*What a twisted, sick woman*, I thought.

A vein in Nik's neck pulsed.

"I don't understand." Knox looked at John. "I've only recently met you. You're definitely not part of Horizon Modeling Agency."

"I'm not part of that puny organization. They're insignificant." John brushed an imaginary piece of lint of his suit. "My boss is the one calling the shots. She hired Horizon to make Viggo comply at any cost, and they would be paid handsomely."

"Why would they go along with that?" Knox kept shaking his head, clearly confused.

"The agency was hurting. They would go along with anything that brought them money." John leveled a stare at Knox. "Everyone has a price. It's amazing what people will do for money. The agency made sure Viggo got hurt and then got him addicted to the pain killers so they could own him." John sneered at Viggo. "He was too humiliated to leave and get help. His pride did him in just like they knew it would."

"But I showed you all when I did walk away." Viggo glared at John. "I'm through with letting them or your boss control me anymore."

John's face hardened. "You should have thought about who you were dealing with before walking away." He laughed harshly. "Everyone knows you don't walk away from my boss. She gets whatever she wants. She's a powerful woman with powerful connections. There's no coming back from that."

Knox backed away with his hands up. "Hey, man, I didn't sign up for this."

John turned his intense eyes on Knox. "You're a coward just like him."

Viggo sneered. "I'm not afraid of your boss or you."

"You should be." John pulled out a knife. "Now where is it?"

Viggo's sneer vanished as he held up his hands. "Where's what?"

"You know what I'm talking about. Where did you hide the pictures? The last ones you were in? My boss will not be happy if that gets leaked."

"I never took anything with me when I left," Viggo responded carefully.

"I don't believe you." John tucked the knife into his jacket and pulled out a gun with a silencer on it. "Knives are quieter, but a gun is less messy." He aimed it at the trio. "I'll ask you one last time. Where is the thumb drive?"

"You killed Delilah, looking for that, didn't you?" Viggo asked, his eyes narrowing. "And now you're planning on killing us for the same reason."

"Smart man. I'm not above killing anyone if I don't get what I want, now hand it over or I'll—"

Nik kicked the door open, yelling, "Police, drop your weapon." His gun was trained on John's chest.

John paused for a long moment as he studied Nik, considered his options, then he finally lowered the gun.

"Wise decision," Nik growled.

"He has a knife in his pocket," Viggo blurted.

"We saw," I replied.

John's eyes locked onto mine. "We meet again, Ms. Ballas. Are you sure you want to get involved in this?"

"Oh, it's too late for that, Mr. Smith." I didn't so much as flinch. "You involved me when you messed with my aunt. I suggest you throw that knife on the bed."

"And the knife strapped to your ankle while you're

at it." Nik's gaze never left John. As soon as the weapons were out of his reach, Nik moved in and handcuffed him.

"Thanks, cuz. I'm glad that's over." Viggo let out a breath.

"Nothing's over, Viggo." Nik shook his head. "You don't get it. You can't keep making mistakes and then just walking away." He looked away from his cousin and back to what he was doing with John as he added, "You still have to answer to breaking into Doc's office and stealing controlled substances."

"What?" Viggo gaped, sounding sincere and drawing all our eyes back to him. "I promise you I never did that. That has to be John trying to set me up."

"Search my room." John's voice was smug. "You won't find any drugs here."

"Of course not. I'm sure they're in my room, but I don't understand. I never let you into my aunt's house, unless..." Viggo turned accusing eyes onto Zelda. "Blackmail is bad enough, Zelda. I can't believe even you would stoop that low."

"You mean he was working a side hustle with you, too?" Knox gaped at Zelda.

"I didn't steal anything." She crossed her arms. "I'm not going down for something he did. John stole the drugs. I just planted them in Viggo's room at his aunt's."

"You just admitted to being an accessory," I pointed out. "That's still a crime."

Her face paled.

"You're not completely innocent, Vig," Nik said solemnly. "You stole from Ma and Kalli's Aunt Tasoula."

"I know." Viggo's voice filled with remorse. "You're

right. I can't keep messing up and then running away. I want to get better. Do better. I need help, Nikos, not jail. I'm finally willing to ask for it."

"You'd better hope neither of them presses charges." Nik blew out a breath and then looked at his cousin, relenting a little. "But I doubt they will. I'll look into a program for you if you want."

"Thank you," Viggo said with sincerity. "That's all I ask."

Nik nodded once before looking at a not-so-smug handcuffed John. "In the meantime, you're under arrest for a whole lot of things, including murdering Delilah Doolittle and Mack Finley." Nik finished reading John his Miranda rights. "Don't try to deny it. We heard you confess."

"You're making a big mistake," John said.

"Tell it to the judge."

The next day after church and Sunday brunch, Jaz and I went wedding dress shopping. Jaz wanted to go to Vixen's because she didn't want anything to do with finding and ordering her own dress. She wanted someone else to measure her, order the gown, and be in charge if anything went wrong.

"I just can't handle being the one to screw up my own dress or yours, if that makes any sense." Jaz looped her arm through mine.

I was her maid of honor and the only one standing up with her, and Nik was Boomer's best man and the only groomsman. It was to be a small intimate affair with their closest friends and family. Of course, now that she was marrying Boomer and leading a more *respectable life*, my family had embraced her. They were having nothing to do with *small* anything, whether she liked it or not.

"I get it. Besides, you deserve the full treatment, and to be pampered for once." I pulled us through the front door of the full-service salon.

The owner of Vixen, Anastasia Stewart, was a tall, chic woman who used to be Jaz's rival, but they had made peace and come a long way. They were actually confidantes about the fashion industry now, since they each had a different flair of their own and different styles to choose from. They'd decided there was room for them both in town.

We were a few minutes early, so we browsed the racks. Lois, Sherry, and Yvonne were there, of course, because Sundays were "sale" days, and Lois always had coupons.

Lois waved and dragged the ladies over to us. "Kalli, Jaz...I'm happy to see you safe and sound. I am *so* relieved the killer has been caught. I mean, poor Dixie. Having your twin sister murdered over a thumb drive of pictures, for goodness sake. And then poor Theresa. Mack was a bad man, but still, having your husband murdered would be my worst nightmare." Lois leaned over and cupped her mouth. "Though, for a hot minute, I thought maybe she had offed the abuser herself."

"It's good to know Clearview's streets are safe again." I said hello to the other women.

"Lois is sending us off with a bang." Sherry clapped. "I just love it here."

"Well, I couldn't let you folks leave before the big sale, now, could I?" Lois beamed. "You want to know what's what, you just ask me."

"Don't forget to stop by Full Disclosure," Jaz added with a wink, making eye contact with all three women. "We have Sunday sales, too."

"I could never forget my favorite store," Lois whispered, looking around the building, "but don't tell Ana."

"I'm pretty sure you say that to all the store owners." Jaz eyed at the women. "Stick with Lois, ladies. Trust me, she has the best coupons in town."

"So, you guys are leaving today?" I turned to Sherry.

"Yes, Bennett and Humphry say it's time to go. There's a big jewelry auction in the city they both want to attend."

"Yes, thank you for sharing your little town with us." Yvonne's lips tipped up slightly. "Your festival certainly was interesting."

"Yes, well, this time of year can be interesting. Glad you enjoyed the carnival. Well, we won't keep you from the sale. It gets pretty competitive around here. Good luck." I waved to them and pulled Jaz with me.

Jaz raised a brow.

I pointed at Dixie who had just entered the store. Jaz went off to talk to Ana while I made a beeline for the antique store owner.

"Hi, Dixie, I'm so glad I ran into you." I gave her a genuine smile.

"Thank you, Kalli. You don't know how relieved I am that Delilah's killer has been arrested. It's been a nightmare."

"Now you can move back into your house and rent out your apartment."

"That's exactly what I plan to do, right after I lay my sister to rest." Her face showed the first genuine emotion I'd seen. "Delilah actually had an amendment to her will, naming me as the beneficiary. It was signed and dated, she just hadn't had a chance to file it yet." Dixie sniffed. "She really did love me and wanted to make sure I was taken care of."

"Oh, I'm so glad you got that worked out."

"All we've had for far too long is each other. I can't believe Andrew really tried to take everything from me, knowing I was Delilah's sister and down on my luck. He never really did love her. He was just selfish. I'm convinced of that now."

So that was why I'd seen Bessie Hallifax with another man just this morning. She must have found out Andrew wasn't getting the money, so she'd already moved on.

"I'm glad things are finally looking up for you. And remember, Jaz and I are around if you ever need anything."

"Thank you, Kalli, that means a lot." Dixie started to walk away. "Oh, hey, will Detective Stevens be free later today? There are a few things I need to take care of, but then I wanted to talk to him about something."

"I'll check with him and see what his schedule looks like and have him give you a call. Will that work?"

"Perfect. Thank you." She looked relieved.

"You're very welcome. Have a good day, Dixie."

"You know? I think I finally will." She smiled and bypassed the sale rack, heading straight for what was hot and new.

LATER THAT DAY I told Nik about what Dixie had said. He promised to give her a call just as soon as he and Boomer finished wrapping up their case. In the meantime, Jaz wanted to look at wedding venues.

They were both overwhelmed with work since the department was still short-staffed. No matter how much the mayor wanted to increase the amount of police on the force, the town didn't have the budget for that. Especially since the Winter Carnival was a bust. Boomer told Jaz to narrow down what she liked, and he would help her choose between the final two.

So, Jaz called me, of course.

Jaz picked me up in her SUV, claiming my Prius wasn't trustworthy, after yesterday's snowstorm, for where we were going. The weather looked good for today, but I wasn't arguing. I hated driving in the snow.

"So where is this place?" I looked out the window.

"I heard about this barn on the outskirts of town that's used for weddings." It's a few miles down this road.

"This is the road that goes past Yanni's landscaping business. I always wondered what was past it. How exciting. Do you think Boomer will like it?"

"Sometimes I think my fiancé was raised in a barn, so he should love it." Jaz laughed. "And if he doesn't, well then, he should have tagged along."

A few minutes later, we came upon Yanni's Yards.

"I didn't know your cousin was open on Sundays?"

"He's not." I frowned, staring at a light on in the greenhouse. "The family would kill him if he missed Sunday brunch or worked on a holy day."

Jaz started pulling off the road into the driveway.

"What are you doing?"

"We need to check this out."

"But what about the barn?"

"It will still be standing when we're done. Your family is my second family. Family comes first." Jaz winked.

"Thank you." I hopped out of her SUV.

There weren't any lights on in the front and no cars. We walked around to the back, and I sighed in relief. Dixie's car was parked near the entrance of the greenhouse. There was a light on as we walked through the door.

"Dixie, what are you doing in here?" I asked.

She jumped and screeched. Her hands were covered in dirt from sticking them in the base of the tree she'd picked out for her yard. "You scared me half to death." She looked guilty of something. I couldn't quite tell what.

"Does Yanni know you're here."

"Oh, yes. I would never come here if he didn't say it was okay." She caught her breath. "I told him there was something I forgot in the greenhouse, but he was too busy to meet me here. He gave me the code and told me it was fine for me to go on my own. Detective Stevens called me. I told him to meet me here. He should be coming soon."

"Okay, I'm confused." It suddenly occurred to me. "Were you looking for a thumb drive of pictures?"

She gave me an odd look. "Why on earth would I put a thumb drive in dirt?"

"I'm not really sure why you would put anything in dirt?" I narrowed my eyes.

"That's what I want to talk to the detective about." Dixie's cheeks were flushed.

"Did you lose a ring or something?" Jaz asked.

"Close...but I didn't lose it. I hid it. I found something, thought it was the answer to my problems, then I panicked and didn't want it anymore, but I didn't know what to do about it. That's why I wanted to talk to the detective." Her eyes met mine and filled with helplessness. "I can't keep this secret any longer."

"It's okay. You don't have to," I said. "We're here now."

"Ladies, my goodness, are you okay?" a male voice came from the doorway.

We whirled around and I tripped, falling to the floor.

"I saw the light on and thought something was

amiss." Bennett rushed over to me and held out a hand while Humphry stood by the door.

"We're fine. I thought you were on your way out of town." I took his hand and let him help me up.

"Sherry and Yvonne already left. Humphry and I got a late start." *I really liked you. Why did you have to be in the wrong place at the wrong time?* He tried to let go, but I held tight to his hand.

"What are you looking for in my cousin's shop, Bennett?"

"I don't know what you're talking about. I simply stopped by to be a good citizen and help." He looked at Dixie. *I didn't mean to do it. It was all her fault. She made me do it.*

"Oh, my Zeus, you killed Delilah." I dropped his hand.

He gaped at me. "H-How did you know?"

Dixie gasped and took a step back. "You're the one who left me that threatening note after breaking into my shop."

"He didn't leave you anything. He's a wimp." Humphry stepped forward. "I did. I'm surprised he had the guts to kill Delilah before I had to come to town and clean up his mess."

"I'm not a killer," Bennett ground out. "This whole thing has gotten out of hand. She made me do it. That wasn't part of the deal."

"Who, Sherry?" I asked, dumbfounded.

"No, me," said a woman's voice from the doorway.

We looked up to see Yvonne standing there, holding a gun pointed at Sherry.

"Bennett, what is happening?" Sherry looked terrified.

"It's okay, honey, just do as they say." Bennett looked genuinely afraid and regretful.

Jaz grabbed my arm and pulled me away from both men. We stood on each side of Dixie, flanking her. Yvonne kept Sherry with her, still having the gun pointed at her.

"They're after the diamonds," Dixie said with certainty.

"What diamonds?" I asked.

"Remember the antique jewelry box I bought at an estate sale? Back in New York City, a wealthy man named Lewis Princeton died."

Sherry gasped, and Bennett closed his eyes.

"Lewis Princeton was my cousin," Sherry said. "My maiden name is Princeton. I thought that jewelry box looked familiar." She shot accusing eyes onto Bennett. "What did you do, Bennett?"

"Like I said, I'm not a killer. I'm a gambler and in debt, which in turn made me become a smuggler. I hid diamonds in the trap door of the jewelry box. Lewis died before I could retrieve them, and his kids didn't know about the trapped door."

"How did you find me?" Dixie asked.

"Lewis's family kept a record of all the sales from the estate sale. I saw your name and the town you were from."

"This wasn't an anniversary trip at all," Sherry said with a sob. "It was a recovery trip."

"I was hoping it was both." Bennett looked down at his feet. "I bought the jewelry box as a gift for you, hoping that would be the end of it, but the diamonds weren't inside."

Sherry wrapped her arms around her middle.

He looked at Dixie. "When you headed out of town, I thought that was my chance. I never imagined your sister would be housesitting." He shook his head, looking ill. "I wasn't sure how I was going to get in until that knife thrower showed up. I hid and watched her find a key in a fake rock, so I slipped inside after her and hid. When she left, I searched for the diamonds, but Delilah caught me in the act. I didn't know what to do. I knew Yvonne wouldn't allow any loose ends, so I just reacted. I grabbed a kitchen knife and tried to make Delilah's death as painless as possible."

"All those years of taking part in fencing matches paid off, I guess. Apparently, you're quite skilled with a knife," Sherry said in disgust. "How did I not wake up when you were gone? You know I'm a light sleeper."

"I gave you sleeping pills." Bennett's face flushed with shame.

Sherry gasped.

"I don't understand where Yvonne and Humphry Rigsby come in," I said.

"He's Rigsby. I'm VanAlstyne," Yvonne said, holding her head high. "I'm Bennett's buyer. Humphry is my employee. He does whatever I need him to whenever I need it, though he's not very good at it."

"Hey." Humphry grunted.

Yvonne shrugged. "You botched killing off Scout after nothing turned up at her trailer. And you didn't even finish searching the pawn shop before that lumberjack showed up."

"Well, I had to take care of him first, and then that maintenance man showed up. What did you expect me to do? Kill him too? You're not as smart as you think you are. You can't kill everyone, Yvonne. That would have drawn too much attention."

"And how do you explain letting Nelson Rockwell live?" Yvonne ground out.

"Because he didn't see me, and his wife came back early." Humphry dusted off his jacket. "I have standards, you know. I draw the line at killing pregnant women."

"Enough of all this chatter." Yvonne cocked her gun. "I hate knives and we're far enough out in the country that I'm comfortable using a gun. I don't need a heavy for that. I'm an expert markswoman."

"What are you going to do?" Bennett asked, his voice wobbling with fear.

Sherry refused to look at him.

"You are of no use to me anymore." Yvonne dragged Sherry with her as she pointed the gun at Dixie, walking all the way over to us, then shoving Sherry by us. Sherry fell by the tree, and I helped her up. I reached down to get my hand sanitizer, forming a plan.

Humphry followed Yvonne's lead and walked over to push Bennett by Sherry.

"But you already paid me half," Bennett sputtered.

"You know too much, and the diamonds are worth much more than I gave you. You were too stupid to know that."

Bennett went to reach for his wife, but Humphry knocked him down.

"You're a fool." Yvonne turned away from him and fixed her eyes on Dixie. "You, my dear, are no fool. You obviously found the diamonds. Clever hiding them in the tree dirt. Now, hand them over. I want what's mine."

"She doesn't have them," I said with my hands cupped together in front of me. "She gave them to me."

"Doesn't matter to me who I kill." Yvonne turned her gun on me.

"They're loose." I raised my cupped together hands. "How do you want them?"

She held out her purse. "Put them in—"

I flung my hands up, straight at her face. Dirt flew into Yvonne's eyes, and she screamed, dropping her gun. Everything happened at once. Bennett tackled Humphry, surprisingly stronger than I'd given him credit for. Jaz pulled Sherry and Dixie out of the way. And I dove for the gun. Rolling to my feet, I lifted the gun and aimed it at Yvonne's chest. Unlike her, I hated guns and did not know how to use one...

But she didn't need to know that.

"Don't move an inch," I said, trying not to let my hands shake.

She called my bluff.

"Why? You know you won't shoot me." She stepped forward.

"No...but I will." Nik cocked his gun as he walked into the room and tossed me his handcuffs. "Nice work, Ballas." His gaze turned hard as he looked at Yvonne. "Cuff her."

"Gladly," I said, thinking we made a pretty darn good team.

# EPILOGUE

"**W**hy are we dressed like this?" Nik asked as he sat next to me on the couch in his living room, wearing a pair of coveralls.

"I'll explain in a minute." I handed him a bottle of water. "Hydrate. You're gonna need it." I took a sip of my own and made conversation while we were waiting. "Aunt Tasoula has her wisdom back."

"Yeah, where did she find it?" Nik took a sip of his water, no questions asked.

Just one of the many things I loved about him.

"She had a cavity. Doc Merigold filled it, and apparently now her wisdom is back in that shiny, tiny new filling."

"I will never understand Greek mamas."

"Speaking of mamas, do you want kids?"

He blinked. "What? Yes, no, I don't know. Where is this coming from?"

"I don't know either, so I guess we'll figure that part out later."

"Later? After what?"

"Not yet. Keep sipping." I took another drink. "So, anyway, Aunt Tasoula is working off her debt to Ma and Pop by working after hours from her salon in their restaurant. Ma is also having her shine Pop's new shoes since she burned his other pairs."

"Oh boy." Nik laughed. "Speaking of your aunt's salon, doesn't Vinny get his hair done there?"

"I know what you're going to say. I saw it, too. His hair is tinted green."

"Okay, so I wasn't imagining things when I saw him earlier. What's up with that?"

"Remember how I told you he called Ma jealous, and she vowed he was gonna be sorry?"

Nik's eyes widened. "She didn't…"

I winced. "I'm pretty sure she did. I saw Ma there the same day, helping Aunt Tasoula out so she could finish early and run deliveries at the restaurant. Ma helped her out, all right. I think she saw an opportunity and took it. Aunt Tasoula accused her of tampering with her hair dye, but Ma claimed to have lost her wisdom. Needless to say, Aunt Tasoula dropped the subject."

"Remind me never to make your ma mad." Nik ran a hand through his hair then took a drink of water. "I found out why Yanni and Senator West have been hanging around each other so much."

This time, I blinked. "Yeah? Why?"

"Yanni is working with Parker to get a scholarship set up in his late girlfriend's name now that he can finally afford it. It's going to be for environmental science majors. I guess Claudett has been very instrumental in helping out. That's what drew them closer."

"Closer?" I smiled with hope.

"Yes, they are actually dating."

"Yay." I pumped my fist through the air.

Nik laughed.

"What about Viggo?" I said gently, not wanting to kill our mood.

"He's going to get the help he needs. He'll have to do some jail time for forging Doc's script, but he'll mostly get help getting clean."

I paused a beat. "Have you forgiven him?"

Nik arched a brow. "For stealing from the fam or stealing from me?"

"Both," I said softly.

Nik sighed. "I will in time."

"Good. Because I don't like seeing you sad."

"*You* make me happy." He winked.

"Well, then, that's all that matters." I kissed his cheek. "What about the thumb drive? That would horrify me, knowing those pictures are floating around out there somewhere."

"Zelda will do time for blackmail and framing Viggo with drugs, while John Smith, his boss, and the agency will answer to their crimes. Knox went back to the city, but no one wants to work with him. Turns out Viggo had the thumb drive stored in his cast all along with all the pictures and proof he needed to sue them for what they did to him. He'll be just fine."

"Well, that's a relief." I thought of something else. "What about Theresa?"

"Turns out she wasn't having an affair. She really just didn't want her shop to become a crime scene. She doesn't want any man and doesn't need one. Mack stored away a lot of money and it all went to her. She's living above her shop and renovating the house Mack abused her in into a shelter for battered women."

"That's amazing. And Sherry? What will happen to her?"

"The diamonds went to Sherry since they were found on her family's property, so she's set and ready to divorce Bennett while he goes to jail for smuggling and murder. Yvonne and Humphry will also go to jail for smuggling, murder, and kidnapping."

"I'm so glad Dixie decided to stick around and give her business another go. You really helped her."

"She should have come forward immediately after discovering the diamonds, but in the end, she did the right thing by contacting me and turning them over. I think she sees Clearview as a place with people who are like family and just want to help." He finished his water. "So, what exactly is this all about?"

I finished my water and bit my bottom lip. "You know those rage rooms where you can go to smash and destroy things in a controlled, safe environment. Like to get all your frustrations out?"

"Yeah, I've seen those before." He grinned. "I heard one opened up in the next town. I've always wanted to do that. Is that where we're going?"

"Yes and no." I stood and motioned him over to me.

He complied, his grin going cockeyed now.

I handed him a pair of safety goggles, and I donned a pair of my own.

"Okay, I'm intrigued." He put his goggles on.

I pulled out two sledgehammers I had hidden behind his table and heaved one at the wall that separated our apartments.

His eyes sprang wide and jaw fell open at the big, gaping hole. I'd started the hole earlier from my side of the house, saving the last dramatic strike for this very moment. "Does this mean what I think it means, Ballas?"

Wolfgang howled as he dove through the hole, giving chase.

Prissy squealed and hissed then took off running.

Nik cursed, and I couldn't help but laugh.

"Welcome to your new life, Detective. There's no turning back now."

# ABOUT THE AUTHOR

Kari Lee Townsend is a National Bestselling Author of mysteries & a tween superhero series. She also writes romance and women's fiction as Kari Lee Harmon. With a background in English education, she's now a full-time writer, wife to her own superhero, mom of 3 sons, 1 darling diva, 1 daughter-in-law & 2 lovable fur babies. These days you'll find her walking her dogs or hard at work on her next story, living a blessed life.

# ALSO BY THE AUTHOR

**Coldwater Cove**

Dark Seas

Frozen Waters

Dangerous Thaw

Deadly Frost

Valley of Secrets

Until Tomorrow

**Merry Scroog-mas**

Naughty or Nice

Sleigh Bells Ring

Jingle all the Way

**Lakehouse Treasures**

James

Amber

Meghan

Brook

**Portrait of a Woman**

Resilient

Love Lessons

Project Produce

**Triple R Ranch**

Destiny Wears Spurs

Spurred by Fate